Pursued by a Dragon

Book II of The Dragon Archives

Linda K. Hopkins

ISBN- **1505430682**
ISBN-13: 978-1505430684

ACKNOWLEDGMENTS

A portion of this book was written while I was visiting South Africa, where I had the opportunity to visit with two very special people. Greta, thank you for all your support and encouragement, and Cathy, your belief in me means more than you can imagine. Thank you.

Of course, there are so many people on this side of the Atlantic who have shared this journey with me. Belinda, thank you for your continued encouragement. Matthew Godden, my patient editor. And of course, my family - Claye, Kristin and Bethany.

A NOTE ABOUT *PURSUED BY A DRAGON*

If you have read *Bound by a Dragon* you already know some of Aaron and Keira's story. But before there was Aaron and Keira, there was Favian and Cathryn! Although this is the second book in *The Dragon Archives*, it predates the first book by a dozen years.

CHAPTER ONE

Cathryn hurried down the muddy street, clutching her packages close to her chest. It was raining, as it had been all week — a slow steady drizzle that stole all color from the landscape and turned the road into a river of sludge, churned by horses and carriages into six inches of mud. Cathryn's leather slippers were completely impractical for these conditions, despite the wooden pattens she had laced onto their soles, and they were covered in mud, as was the hem of her gown. She pulled her skirts up higher and carefully adjusted the packages in her arms. It was at that precise moment that a careless passerby, shoving through the unhappy throng, knocked her off balance, sending one of her parcels spilling out of her arms, straight for the mire. She grabbed at the package, but no sooner had she re-established her grasp on it, than the other tumbled from her grip. Wrapped in coarse hessian and string, it had almost reached the mud when a hand, stretching from behind, snatched the package from its sorry fate. Turning around, Cathryn slowly raised her gaze to look into a pair of blue eyes, deep as bottomless pools reflecting the wide expanse of the heavens. The man towered over her, and although most people towered over Cathryn's five feet, two and a half inches, this man was well past six feet tall, and with a broad chest to match. Adding to the impressiveness of his figure was a head of blazing red hair, hanging loose to his shoulders. He was clean shaven, but looked every bit of what Cathryn supposed a Viking would look like. Not that she had ever seen one of the marauding barbarians, but like anyone else in town, she had heard tales of the violence and sacrilege that had been perpetrated by the invaders up and down the coastline in days gone by. She stared at him, her mouth dropping open, as she took in his features.

"Are you all right, Mistress?" the man asked her gently, the concern in his expression deepening. Cathryn blushed, suddenly aware of how rude, or stupid, she must appear to this stranger. Snapping her mouth closed, she nodded.

"Yes, thank you."

"Where is your attendant?" The man glanced around, his gaze searching out a careless servant, but when he found none, he turned questioning eyes back to her.

Cathryn shrugged. "I am quite unattended."

"It is not safe for a lady to walk these streets alone," he responded, concern creating furrows between thick, heavy eyebrows.

"Thank you for your concern, Sir, but my safety is my own affair!" She paused for a moment to soften her tone before continuing. "Besides, it is broad daylight, and I am well known to my fellow townsmen. I do not believe they would do me harm."

A look of surprise crossed the man's face at Cathryn's sharp retort, but it quickly smoothed over, with just a hint of a grin lurking around his eyes.

"Ah, you may trust the townsmen, but what about strangers who happen within the gates? Do you trust that you are safe with them abroad? Anybody could enter the city during daylight hours — pickpockets, murderers, and ravishers of lovely maidens."

Tipping her head, Cathryn looked at him askance, her eyes narrowed as she regarded him for a moment.

"Into which of these categories do you place yourself, Sir? For I do not recognize your face, which indicates to me that you must be a stranger." In bold perusal, she swept her gaze over his large form, before returning to his now grinning countenance. "You are too well dressed to be a pickpocket, and too well spoken to be a murderer, so perhaps you are a ravisher of maidens. Should I sound the alarm?"

The man grinned appreciatively before leaning in a little closer, his voice dropping slightly.

"None of those things, Mistress. I'm only here to assist a damsel in distress."

"Ah, a knight, then."

The man pulled back and met her gaze. "If that is what you wish. And my first duty as your personal knight will be to escort you to your destination."

"No, no, Sir Knight. You have already performed one service for me, which is as much as a damsel can expect on any given day. So I will relieve you of my package and bid you good day."

Tugging the delinquent parcel from his grasp, she tucked it under her arm before glancing once more into his face. It was clear that he was not happy with her decisive dismissal, but was too much the gentleman to insist. Amused, Cathryn stepped past him to resume her journey along the muddy lane. Instead of watching the path, she kept her eyes warily on the crowds around her, but that proved to be her undoing. Stepping onto a smooth slick of mud, her foot slipped out from under her as her rear end fell towards the morass. She gasped as the packages flew from her hands, her scrabbling feet unable to find purchase on the slippery surface, but before she hit the ground strong hands caught her under the arms and unceremoniously returned to her feet. The packages did not survive the fall, and they lay in the oozing mud as people hurriedly stepped around them. She turned slowly, composing her features, and glanced up, unsurprised to see the large stranger towering above her once more. His warm hands were clamped to the top of her arms, but they fell to his sides as she looked at him.

"How did you reach me so fast?" she asked in surprise. "Or were you following me?"

"I have fast reflexes," he replied with a wry smile. "And I had a feeling you would need my help again!" Cathryn blushed, but did not look away.

"Thank you. But I trust I won't need your services again."

The man grinned as he replied. "I wouldn't be too sure of that. And this time I insist that you allow me to attend you to your destination."

Cathryn opened her mouth to protest, before closing it again slowly. Perhaps it would be foolish to refuse his aid, since he had already assisted her twice, and furthermore, she thought in silent appreciation, he was a very handsome man, and his presence could be an enjoyable diversion.

"Very well," she said with a nod.

"Favian Drake at your service," he said with a small incline of his head. "And may I have the pleasure of knowing your name?"

"Cathryn Forrester," she replied. Favian bent down to retrieve one of the packages that had become buried in the mud, and he turned it over with a frown.

"I trust this did not contain anything of value, Mistress," he said. "I'm afraid whatever was in here is completely ruined!"

"A package of ribbons. I will try washing them, but they are easily replaced," she said as they turned to walk down the road, Favian walking close to Cathryn. His enormous

4

height was a deterrent to other passers-by, who gave him a wide berth.

"You would make a most admirable protector, Sir," Cathryn said, watching the people with interest.

"I'm happy to offer my services," he replied with a grin. Cathryn looked at him in amusement.

"That sounds like a proposition, Sir Knight. Should I be offended?"

"No, no, of course not," Favian replied hastily, his face momentarily aghast. Cathryn laughed at his shocked expression.

"Then I won't take offence!" she said, laughing again at his expression of exaggerated relief.

As they walked along, Cathryn glanced at her protector from under lowered eyes. She had no doubt that the man could hold his own in a fight, even one unevenly matched against him. Through the thin fabric of his tunic she could see that his arms were well muscled and strong. His chest was broad, but his waist was narrow, without the extra padding men often started to sport as they settled into life lived comfortably. She guessed him to be in his early thirties, and wondered whether he was settled with a wife and family. Perhaps he really was a knight, returned from crusades in distant lands, who had never had the time to marry. The man was talking again, and she looked up to meet his gaze. He was smiling as he talked, but there was a firmness around his mouth, and a tightness around his eyes, that suggested he was used to giving orders and expecting them to be followed. Someone who would stand his ground and never back down. A man who would be a loyal friend and an unrelenting enemy.

"Wouldn't you agree, Mistress?"

The questioning tone pulled her from her reflections as she realized that she had not heard a word of what he was saying.

"Mmm," she responded vaguely, determined to pay

LINDA K. HOPKINS

closer attention, when the sound of a yell on the other side of the street drew her notice. Turning to look, her heart sank as she took in the scene. Crawling on the ground, his knees caked in mud, a man was scrambling to collect a pile of kindling that had broken free of its bindings and scattered into the mire, over him stood Geoffrey Beaumont, his hands raised as he berated the man.

"You stupid fool," shouted Geoffrey, the sound of his voice drawing the attention of others. "You could have tripped me into the mud."

"I'm sorry, Master," mumbled the laborer. "I didna see you."

"Next time, look where you are going, you idiot, and make sure you pay attention to your betters."

The public display did not surprise Cathryn. Geoffrey thought little of his peers and still less of his inferiors. She could feel Favian stiffen besides her, watching the scene, and she glanced at him, catching his look of derision. He opened his mouth to make some comment, but before he could say anything, she quickly took the soggy packages from his hands.

"Thank you for your help, Sir Knight. It is not far from here, so I will relieve you of my company and bid you good day." Cathryn glanced over her shoulder, relieved to see that Geoffrey still had not noticed her.

For reasons she did not even try to understand, she did not want Favian Drake to learn that Geoffrey Beaumont was her betrothed. It was not, after all, a relationship to be ashamed of. Her betrothal to Geoffrey had been negotiated by her father and was based on a business partnership, and had little to do with personal affection. It was quickly becoming clear, however, that she was not to get her wish. Not only was Favian making no moves to leave her side, but another glance over her shoulder showed her that Geoffrey had finally seen her, and was pushing a path through the crowd towards them. A meeting was inevitable.

6

Sighing, Cathryn turned to face Favian once more.

"You are about to meet my betrothed," she said. For a moment Favian looked confused, but it quickly turned to a look of contempt as Geoffrey stepped before them.

"Cathryn, whatever are you doing on these ghastly streets?" Geoffrey gave her a quick glance before looking at the man at her side. Favian had taken a step closer, a strangely protective gesture that gave Cathryn a twist in her stomach. Before she could respond, Favian inclined his head towards the newcomer.

"Favian Drake at your service." Standing so close to him, Cathryn could feel the heat rising from Favian's skin, but his voice was cold and she shivered involuntarily.

"Favian Drake? I know that name," said Geoffrey, his brows furrowed as he tried to place it.

"And you are …?"

Geoffrey started in surprise before his eyes narrowed in speculation. "Geoffrey Beaumont, Mistress Cathryn's betrothed," he said slowly.

Favian nodded, meeting his glance for a brief moment before turning in Cathryn's direction. His eyes lacked the warmth they had held before, while his manner was decidedly aloof. He gave her a shallow bow.

"Good day, Mistress." Turning on his heel, he walked away without a backward glance.

CHAPTER TWO

Cathryn lifted her skirts as she stepped over the pungent piles of horse dung that decorated the street. Flies rose into the air, and she swatted at them in revulsion before they settled back down on the brown heaps. Up ahead she could see a pair of street cleaners leaning on their shovels and laughing over some joke. Cathryn returned her attention to the minefield ahead of her, remembering the accident she had escaped only a few days before. She smiled, her mind lingering on the memory of Favian Drake. The man was not easily forgotten, and indeed had made his way into her thoughts more often than was probably right for a woman betrothed to another man. It was not his size that kept him in her mind, although that was impressive; nor his looks, as handsome as they were. It was his smile she remembered, the concern he had shown for her in Geoffrey's presence. The heat that emanated from his skin, the look in his eyes, the touch of his hands. She caught herself in her musings, blushing at where her thoughts had been taking her.

She pushed all thoughts of Favian Drake away from her mind as her father's warehouse rose up ahead of her. Stepping without hesitation into the large brick building, she nodded at the men working on the floor before lifting her skirts and climbing the rickety stairs that led to Father's office. This warehouse had been her childhood playground, and she had first learned to walk and climb within these walls. As she grew older, she had sat with her father as he explained the wool business to her. She learned her letters by reading contracts, and lessons in mathematics had been conducted when she carefully added the numbers in the ledger. By the time she was twelve years old she was learning the intricate subtleties of negotiation, sitting in on meetings with the exporters who sent the wool across the waters to be sold to foreign cloth merchants. And as a teenager, she had accompanied her father as he visited grand estates, austere monasteries and town markets, searching out the best supplies of wool and negotiating contracts. Now, at the age of five and twenty, she knew as much about the wool business as her father. She was well known amongst the workers in the warehouse and had earned the respect of other wool merchants. And although not a member of the wool merchant's guild, or Company, as it was known, it was understood that she would step into that role when she took over control of the business from Master Forrester.

Cathryn greeted her father with a nod as she entered the bare office at the top of the stairs, seating herself at a small high table that stood opposite the large desk where he sat.

"Good morning Cathryn," he said. "I have placed a missive recently received from our friends in Bruge on your desk. Please review it and let me know your thoughts. Also, there is a letter from our bankers which needs a response. I will leave that in your hands to reply as you see fit."

Cathryn nodded. "Very good, Father," she said as she pulled up a seat and settled herself down to work.

It was mid-afternoon by the time Cathryn left the warehouse, leaving her father to continue working. The streets were wet from a recent spring shower but had,

Cathryn was pleased to note, been cleared of the waste that littered the streets that morning. The streets were still uncrowded, and shopkeepers greeted her with a smile as she walked past. She glanced across the street, and almost stopped when she saw Favian Drake on the opposite side of the road, engaged in conversation with another man. His companion was also very tall, she noticed, but perhaps not quite as tall as Favian, nor as broad. He had golden brown hair that had been pulled into a queue at the back of his neck, and his hand rested on Favian's arm in a gesture of familiarity. She glanced away again, picking up her pace, but not before she saw Favian lift his head and slowly turn in her direction.

"Mistress Cathryn," she heard. Her heart quickened at the sound of his voice, and she looked up to see Favian Drake crossing the road as he came towards her, his companion having disappeared.

"Master, uh …"

"Drake," he supplied. "Favian Drake."

"Ah, yes. Master Drake." She smiled sheepishly. Even she could hear the lie in her voice.

"Still walking unattended, I see," he said, falling into step beside her.

"I don't have far to go," she explained.

"And no packages, either. I was hoping to offer my services, but it would appear you have no need of them."

She glanced at him, flushing when she caught his amused smile. "You are laughing at me," she said.

"Well, yes," he admitted. This time it was his turn to look sheepish. She tried to frown at him, but her sense of humor got the better of her, and she laughed.

"That is very ungentlemanly of you."

"Yes, I confess it is," he replied, his eyes holding hers as he returned her smile. She pulled her gaze away, quietly drawing in a deep breath to still her racing heart.

"Do you often spend time at your father's warehouse?"

he asked.

"How did you —?"

"I asked some friends about you. I understand that you are quite involved in the family business."

"You were asking after me? Why?"

"You intrigued me. I wanted to know more about you."

"Oh. And what did you find out?"

"I found out that you are involved in your father's business."

"Well, that gives you an unfair advantage. You know something about me, while I know nothing about you."

"I'm happy to share all my secrets with you," he said. "Well," he amended, "some of my secrets, at least for now. Will you allow me to call on you?"

"No," she said, aghast. "I can't allow that. You already know I am betrothed to another man."

"Ah, yes. Geoffrey Beaumont. I've been asking about him, too." He stopped, and she glanced around to see they were already outside her house. "I also found out where you live," he said in response to her unspoken question. He glanced up at the house, his eyes lingering on the window on the upper floor. Like most houses in town, its frame was of thick oak, now darkened with age, filled with a mixture of wattle and daub. The upper storey overhung the street by a few feet, and it was here that Cathryn had her chambers, with the multi-paned leaded window overlooking the street.

Favian turned back to Cathryn. "I look forward to our next chance encounter," he said. "Good day." He nodded his head and turned on his heel before she had a chance to reply. She watched his retreating figure with a mixture of dismay and amusement.

"Hannah," she said later that evening as her lady's maid carefully brushed out her hair, "do you believe in love at first sight?" She regretted the question as soon as it left her mouth.

"Love at first sight?" Hannah repeated. "That is not a question I would have expected *you* to ask, Mistress."

"I know," she groaned. "I don't know where it came from. Please pay it no mind."

"You've met someone, haven't you?"

"No," Cathryn said. "No," she repeated more firmly. "I am betrothed to Geoffrey Beaumont. I do not even believe in love, as well you know. All love does is lead you into misery. And all those romantic notions you hear of in tales and songs …" Cathryn shuddered. "Pure foolishness."

"Hmm." Hannah pulled the brush through Cathryn's hair a few more times, making it gleam in the candlelight. "So, who is he?"

"No-one. He is no-one." Cathryn closed her eyes when she saw Hannah's raised eyebrows in the mirror. "He's a man I met on the street. A nobody. But I cannot get him out of my mind."

"Handsome, is he?"

"Yes, but that's not it. There's something about him; I cannot even say what it is. But his memory unsettles me and leaves me feeling very …" — it took a moment to find the right word — "… dissatisfied. Perhaps," she continued, turning to face Hannah, "I should start planning my wedding to Geoffrey. We've been betrothed for, how many years has it been?"

"Three. But rushing your wedding won't solve anything," Hannah warned.

"Nonsense, it will be the perfect distraction. You will help me, of course," she said, turning back to face the mirror.

"Perhaps you should discuss this with Master Beaumont before you post the banns," Hannah suggested as she pulled Cathryn's hair into a tight braid.

"I suppose you are right," she said. "And Hannah, lay out my habit, please. I think I will go for an early morning ride."

CHAPTER THREE

Cathryn sat in the small parlor that led off from the great hall, her back straight in the hard-backed chair, looking at Geoffrey as he sat across from her.

"I was thinking we should select a date in the winter," Cathryn was saying. "Spring and summer are far too busy —"

"Why this sudden urgency?" Geoffrey interjected. "You have never shown any inclination to rush into marriage before. In fact, one of the reasons I was happy to enter into this contract with you is because you are usually so reasonable, unlike many others of your sex."

"Why, thank you," Cathryn said dryly, "but I would hardly call three years a rush."

"No, of course not," Geoffrey responded, "but you have to admit this is all rather sudden. I thought we were quite content to leave our situations unchanged for the present time. Both our businesses have already benefited from this alliance, and formalizing the marriage now won't alter anything."

Presented with this logic, Cathryn found she had no argument. After all, it was the success of the business that had directed every major decision she had ever made before now.

"Perhaps I just want to be married," she said, aware that she sounded petulant. Geoffrey stared at her in disbelief, before bursting into a hoot of cynical laughter.

"Whatever the reason for this nonsense," he said between laughs, "it is not because you want to settle into the tedium of married life. Before you start arranging this wedding, be sure that you really want to follow this route at the present time."

"Fine," she ground out as Geoffrey continued to laugh at her. She stood up, irritated, and turned to look out the window as the door opened and Father walked into the room.

"Ah, Cathryn, I've been looking for you, but I see you are presently engaged." He nodded to Geoffrey before returning his attention to his daughter. "Please find me when you have a moment."

"Yes, Father. Is it a matter of urgency?"

"Nothing that cannot wait a few hours. It is regarding our annual tour of suppliers, but we can discuss it later." Nodding once more in Geoffrey's direction, he exited the room.

Cathryn turned to look at Geoffrey. The humor was still evident in his face, but he had a roll of paper in his hand, which he was spreading out on a desk near the window.

"As entertaining as this discussion has been, my dear, I actually came here to discuss a matter of business. Come look at these figures," he said, pointing to a column of numbers written with ink on the scroll of thick linen paper. "As you know, demand for our woolens and worsteds is growing, which means that we need to acquire larger quantities of both long-haired and short-haired wool." Pulling her chair closer, Cathryn bent over the numbers with Geoffrey, the previous conversation giving way to the weightier matters of business.

The light was already beginning to fade when Cathryn found her father some hours later, bent over a pile of papers, on which she recognized the seal of a fellow-merchant.

"Come in, Cathryn," Father said, gesturing her into the room. "Sit down." Cathryn waited as he finished making some notes before carefully wiping his quill and placing it in a holder on the desk. "I need you to go on the road without me this year." Cathryn nodded. This was not completely unexpected. "The king wants to raise taxes," he continued, "and the Company will, of course, be sending a delegation to negotiate some concessions." As a leading member of the wool merchant's guild, it was to be expected that Father would join the delegation. "Perhaps we can negotiate a lifting of the current trade embargo, a benefit to us that will also further enrich the royal coffers," he added wryly. "The delegation plans to leave as soon as possible, and I do not want to delay our tour of estates, since heaven only knows how long these negotiations may drag on for.

"Of course," continued Father, "you won't be traveling alone. Felix will travel with you, and you can take whatever personal staff you feel you will require."

Cathryn nodded. She knew that Felix, her father's trusted bailiff and Hannah's grandfather, would form part of the retinue. Older than her father by a few years, Felix had served as a trusted employee for as long as Cathryn could remember. He was a man of few words, but he had always had a friendly regard for Cathryn. She knew she would be quite safe traveling the countryside with him, and although most suppliers were familiar with her by now, his presence would also ensure they would treat her with more respect than if she were alone.

"Very well, Father." Cathryn nodded. "I will start making the necessary arrangements, and trust that your negotiations with the king will be successful."

"I believe we can come to a suitable arrangement with His Royal Highness," said Father with a slight smile. He looked at her more closely for a moment before continuing. "Is everything all right between you and Geoffrey? You seemed a little out of sorts when I interrupted you this afternoon."

"It was nothing, Father," Cathryn replied with a slight grimace. "It appears we do not share the same sense of humor, nothing more."

"Well, a good marriage is not dependent on a shared sense of humor," said Father, returning his attention to his papers.

CHAPTER FOUR

It was a lovely day, full with the promise of spring. New leaf buds, their color still a delicate green, were exploding on the trees, while blossoms shyly paraded their soft hues for all the world to see. Cathryn, standing just inside the open front door, took in a deep breath, filling her lungs with the scent of early morning. The air was still fresh and untouched by the heat of day which would later ripen the smells into a more pungent mélange. She patted her waist, assuring herself that the purse which hung from her belt was in place, before setting out through the door. As she walked she reviewed the list of items she sought, numbering them to aid her memory. It was the midweek market day, which brought with it merchants and craftsmen who traveled from farther afield with their wares. The purchase of kitchen fare was left to the household servants, but Cathryn had a few personal items she wanted to purchase: a hairpin to replace the one that had fallen into the fire grate earlier in the week, a new quill with a delicately curling feather, and ribbons to replace those that had been ruined in the mud a few weeks before. Thought of the ruined ribbons immediately brought to mind the man who had rescued her from the mire, but she resolutely pushed the thought away, turning back to her list. She needed more sheets of paper, and leather thongs to bind them with, and she had heard that one of the merchants had obtained bangles crafted with intricately designed silver filigree, from the Emerald Isle.

It was not far to the town market, and a few minutes later saw Cathryn standing before a table that held a colorful array of ribbons.

"Need more ribbons already, Mistress?" asked the young woman behind the table with a smile. Cathryn was a familiar face to the townspeople, and as she always brought with her a cheerful greeting, and never begrudged a merchant a fair price, she was treated with more affection than some of the other well-born ladies of the town. Cathryn returned the smile as she fingered the bright hanks, mulling over the selection of reds, oranges and yellows.

"I'm afraid the last package was ruined in the mud," she said. She leaned over the table, examining the bright hues.

"Oh, that's too bad," the woman responded. "I'm afraid I don't have any more green ribbon, but I do have some lovely blue which I will show you." She scratched around under the table, pulling out a hank of sapphire-blue ribbon.

"I'll take it," Cathryn said immediately.

It took her a few more minutes to complete her selection and pay the young woman before she moved off in the direction of a merchant displaying a selection of quills. She glanced around as she walked, taking note of the crowds of shoppers, when a tall form caught her attention. He was turned away from her, but the red hair, gleaming in the morning sun, gave him away. Cathryn felt the breath catch in her throat as she looked at the man who had haunted her memories, before quickly turning in the opposite direction in a panic. The man roused within her a yearning she had never before experienced, a desire that threatened all she held to be true. She had covered quite a few hurried yards before she forced her pace to slow down, chagrined at her instinctive response to run. Adopting a far more sedate pace, she crossed the last few yards to where the jewelry merchant displayed his wares. Silver glittered in the sunlight, and she stroked the smooth surfaces, her finger tracing the delicate swirls and curves, before choosing one with a pattern of trailing flowers and slipping it onto her wrist. Holding out her hand, she twisted it this way and that, watching the metal sparkle against her fair skin.

"This one, I think."

A voice, soft and masculine, startled her, as a hand reached around her and lifted another bangle from the dark-colored cloth of the table. Cathryn knew without turning who it was that stood behind her. The voice had pursued her through many dreams, and as his warm breath brushed against her hair, she felt her heart speed up and the blood pound in her ears. For a brief moment she closed her eyes, silently pulling in extra breath, before slowly turning around to face him.

"Sir, er, Drummond, was it?" she said. She glanced up into his face, before quickly looking away again.

"Drake," he corrected. He looked at her with eyes narrowed. "But you knew that. I saw you rushing across the market in an effort to avoid me. Now why would you do that, I wonder?"

Cathryn raised startled eyes to meet his. "That is a very arrogant assumption. Why would I want to avoid you?"

"Why indeed? Is it because your thoughts have bent towards me more than you care to admit?" He held her gaze for a moment, then glanced down at the bangle in his hand. Intricate lines of silver twisted and curled around each other, in a never-ending pattern that looped around the bangle between bands of silver. Pulling her hand into his, he gently tugged the bangle she still wore off her wrist and replaced it with the one he had chosen.

"There," he said, "that suits you perfectly. Small and dainty, but with a strong and determined design." He watched her as she frowned down at the piece of jewelry adorning her wrist, her expression wavering between approval and chagrin. Finally, digging into her purse, she pulled out a few coins and handed them to the merchant before turning away.

"Aren't you going to thank me?" he asked, falling into step beside her.

"Thank you?"

"Yes. For finding you the perfect piece to complement your graceful wrist."

"You are insufferable," she said, annoyed. Annoyed at him, for making her indebted to him. And even more at herself, for being affected by him.

"How is your betrothed?" he said. "Shouldn't he be here, attending to you, showing his affection and showering you with gifts?"

She took a deep breath before replying. "My marriage to Geoffrey Beaumont has nothing to do with affection," she said, lifting her chin as she responded. "It is a business partnership, nothing more. Not," she added, "that it concerns you in the least."

"A business partnership," he mused. "Do you have no feelings for the man?"

"Of course I do," she retorted. "I admire his business sense and respect his intelligence."

"Ah. A fine foundation for a successful marriage. Is there no-one that you love, then? One with whom you share mutual affection?"

"No. I have seen love make fools of my friends, and I choose not to go down that road. Nor have I ever been tempted to."

She carried on for a few more steps, glancing at Favian when he didn't reply. His face wore an expression of deep consideration, but it cleared as he returned her look.

"Good day, Mistress," he said with a small bow. "I will leave you to your perusals."

Cathryn nodded, staring after him as he turned away and strode through the crowd. Clearly her words had made him leave. What was not clear, however, was why she felt so bereft. She was still pondering this when he glanced back over his shoulder, his gaze catching hers for a moment before he turned back and disappeared between the masses.

CHAPTER FIVE

Hannah bustled around the room as Cathryn lay in a tub of warm water, the scent of roses rising from the crushed petals that had been strewn into the bath.

"I'm thinking the green gown, Mistress," said the young woman, "trimmed in silver."

"Perfect," Cathryn said, lathering soap over her arms as she answered. She was looking forward to an evening spent at the Bradshaws'. Thomas Bradshaw was a fellow merchant and a great friend of her father's, while his wife, Elise, was a kind, motherly woman. Twice each year the couple held a great feast, where they offered entertainment in the form of traveling troubadours and musicians. This year, Father had informed her, Elise had even managed to find a bard to end the evening's entertainment with a tale or two.

A pail of steaming water stood next to the tub, and hefting it Hannah poured the water over Cathryn in a gentle stream. She held out a large linen sheet as Cathryn rose out of the water. Fetching a small bottle of colored glass from the chest of drawers, she rubbed attar of rose over Cathryn's smooth skin, rubbing in vigorous circles over her shoulders and neck.

"Will a certain gentleman be there this evening?" Hannah asked.

"Geoffrey? I don't believe so," Cathryn said. "He does not enjoy this kind of entertainment." She smiled at Hannah's look of indignation.

"That is not the gentleman I was referring to."

"Then I cannot imagine to whom you could be referring," said Cathryn. "Thinking of any man other than my betrothed would be most improper."

"Very well," Hannah said. "I will not press you any further."

An hour had sped past by the time Cathryn emerged from her bedchamber, a silk cloak thrown over her dark green gown. The hair around her face had been braided with silver ribbons, while the rest hung loose over her shoulders and flowed down her back. On her wrist she wore the filigree bangle that Favian had selected for her, the pattern curving in an intricate design that caught the light. Silver slippers covered her feet, peeking from beneath her gown as she quickly made her way down the stairs to where her father was awaiting her.

"Ready?" said Father, holding out his arm when she nodded her agreement.

The Bradshaw family lived only a few streets away, and Cathryn and Father were soon ambling down the street in that direction, forgoing the carriage and instead traveling on foot. It was a lovely evening, the waxing moon shining brightly in the night sky. When they arrived at the house they were quickly ushered into the hall. The room was long, running the length of the house, with a high, beamed ceiling that soared above them. Rush torches were interspersed at regular intervals along the walls, creating light that danced and shimmied in the moving air. A huge fire roared in a hearth set in one of the long walls, while at the far end of the hall was a raised dais on which stood a covered table that ran the width of the room. There was a screen behind the table, half hiding the musicians seated behind it, some of whom strummed on lutes and citoles, while others accompanied them on timbrels. More tables flanked with benches ran along the length of the hall, stopping a few yards short of the dais.

As Cathryn and her father entered the room, they were greeted by Thomas and Elise Bradshaw. Within moments, Thomas and Father were deep in conversation about the upcoming delegation to the king, while Cathryn and Elise shared an amused smile.

"Come in, Cathryn," said Elise, waving her into the room. "Most of the younger people are over there," she said, gesturing to a crowd of people at the far end of the hall. "Why don't you go and join them."

"Thank you," Cathryn said with a smile. The group of people were laughing, and as Cathryn approached she saw that most of the crowd were familiar to her. A tall, willowy woman, strikingly dressed in a crimson gown, glanced over her shoulder; observing Cathryn's approach, she walked over and hooked her arm through her friend's.

"Peggy," Cathryn said by way of a greeting.

"You have to come meet this most interesting man," Peggy said softly, pulling Cathryn into the circle. "He has just returned from travels abroad, and has been entertaining us with some stories." The bustle of Cathryn's arrival in the group attracted the attention of the man seated in the center, and he paused to glance up at the newcomer. As Cathryn turned to look at the stranger, dark blue eyes met hers, sparkling with amusement; she felt her eyes widen in surprise.

"Cathryn, this is Favian Drake," announced Peggy. "Master Drake," she said, turning to Favian, "this is Mistress Cathryn Forrester." Cathryn stared at the man sitting before her, the color rushing to her cheeks as Favian's mouth stretched into a slow smile. Pushing himself to his feet, he made a small bow in Cathryn's direction before turning to the people around him.

"Mistress Cathryn and I are already acquainted," he announced to the circle. "In fact," he added mischievously, casting a quick glance in Cathryn's direction, "we became quite well acquainted when I rescued her, uh, derriere, from becoming too familiar with the mud!"

There was a ripple of laughter through the group as Cathryn fought the blush that rose to her cheeks.

"Really?" Peggy said, laughing. "You didn't tell me, Cathryn!"

"There wasn't really anything to tell," Cathryn said with an airy wave of her hand. "The incident was barely worth remembering. My packages were quite ruined, so everything else was forgotten."

Turning to Favian, she gave him a sly look. "So it was you who was my rescuer, Master, er, Drake? My apologies, I had quite forgotten." She grinned as Favian gave a mocking salute of defeat. "Now if you will excuse me, I am in desperate need of some libation." Turning on her heel, Cathryn walked away, her hands trembling slightly as she tried to calm her chaotic thoughts. Behind her she could hear her friends laughing, while someone chaffed Favian at his put-down.

A long passage ran down the length of the hall, leading to the kitchens at the back of the house. There were numerous doorways between the passage and hall, and it was to one of these that Cathryn made her way now, cup of wine in hand, as she sought a moment's privacy to regain her composure. She had just stepped into the passage when she felt warm fingers curl around her arm. Startled, she glanced around, relaxing only slightly when she saw who it was tugging her towards a small nook in the passage.

"Oh, it's you," she said.

"Yes, you do remember me, don't you?" Favian asked. The passage was dingy, with the light from the hall providing the only illumination, but even so, she could see the flash of his eyes as he spoke. They seemed to be glowing with a faint yellow light, and she stared up at him, fascinated. His hand was still on her arm, and he gently stroked her skin, his warmth spreading through her at his touch. Glancing down, he circled his other hand around her wrist below the bangle, before meeting her gaze once more.

"You were very rude," she whispered.

"Yes," he said, "I was. I was curious to see whether you would deny knowing me yet again. I was sure you would, and as it turned out, I was correct." He trailed his finger around her wrist, and she shivered. "I have a theory as to why you keep denying me," he said. His eyes seemed to glow even more as he leaned closer to her, the heat from his body touching hers. Her back was against the wall, and she pushed herself against the cool surface, trying to create some distance between them, but he followed her, bending his mouth towards her ear.

"I think it is a futile attempt to put me out of your mind," he said softly. "I think the memory of me pursues you at every turn, just as yours does me. Am I right?"

No, Cathryn wanted to scream, but she could not make the falsehood form on her lips. Instead she stared at him mutely as he watched her.

"I thought so," he said, with a note of satisfaction. He pulled back to gaze into her eyes for another brief moment before turning away and walking back to the hall. Leaning back against the wall, she closed her eyes, drawing in deep breaths in an effort to still her racing heart. *The man is relentless,* she thought. If he would just leave her alone, she could push him from her mind and forget about him. She took a deep gulp of wine before turning back towards the room.

She hadn't taken more than a few steps when Peggy appeared at her side.

"Why didn't you tell me about your encounter with

Favian Drake?" she demanded. Cathryn shrugged.

"As I said before, there was nothing to tell. I find I have absolutely no interest in the man."

The man in question was on the other side of the room, his back to them, and Cathryn glanced at him as she spoke. Her voice was low, but even so, he turned to look at her, his eyebrows raised questioningly. He held her gaze across the room for a moment, before turning away again.

"Absolutely no interest whatsoever," repeated Cathryn, dropping her voice even lower. Once again he glanced up to look at her. Peggy, who had missed the exchange, was speaking again, and Cathryn pulled her attention away from Favian to follow what she was saying.

"So you don't mind if I get to know him better?"

"Peggy, you can do as you please," Cathryn said. "It is nothing to me. Besides," she added as an afterthought, "I am already promised to Geoffrey."

"Good!" Half amused and half annoyed, Cathryn watched Peggy as she stared openly at Favian before turning away, making a direct path to a table with a full jug of wine.

CHAPTER SIX

Cathryn ignored Favian all evening, even slipping out the side door when she saw him approaching, an action that gave her a flash of mortification. So when she took her place on the bench at supper, she was dismayed to find that he was sitting on the opposite side, just a little further down. Peggy had remained glued to his side for the entire evening, and she took a seat next to him on the bench, throwing a triumphant smile at her friend.

Someone dropped down on the bench next to Cathryn, and turning towards the newcomer, Cathryn forced a weak smile as she greeted Sally Peterson. The woman wriggled about on the bench in an effort to get comfortable on the hard surface, her ample thighs pressing warmly against Cathryn's legs. Sally Peterson was an authority on everything that happened within the town walls, and it was not long before she was regaling everyone within earshot of the latest town events.

"Her father marched her right down to the magistrate to demand a whipping, while her mother wailed and screamed behind him the whole way." Sally took a sip of wine, enjoying the moment of suspense. "The little minx just ignored them both, and walked all the way of her own accord. She refused to name the young man involved, and in my humble opinion, I think it is shameful that he would allow her to take all the punishment while he runs and hides."

Personally, Cathryn had to agree with this sentiment, although she kept her feelings to herself. She glanced across at Favian, watching as he bent his head down to catch something that Peggy was saying. He certainly wasn't discouraging her advances, Cathryn noticed. She was about to look away when he glanced up, meeting her eyes momentarily. He gave a slight nod of acknowledgment before once more turning his attention to Peggy, bringing his head even closer to hers. Cathryn ground her teeth as she turned away. The man clearly was not worth her notice.

The meal finally dragged to an end, and the tables were pushed away to make space in the hall for dancing. As the music filled the large room, Cathryn was quickly pulled into the circle of dancers, where she joined the complicated steps as the line of dancers weaved around the hall, their steps taking them past the town matrons seated sedately on benches pushed against the wall. She noticed Favian dancing beside Peggy at one point, his hand loosely holding hers, but the next time she saw him, he was holding the hand of young Anne Bradshaw, smiling into her eager face. Cathryn watched him as he danced, observing the graceful way he moved despite his size. His flaming hair had been caught in a ribbon at the nape of his neck, and it gleamed a ruddy gold in the glow of the torches that lit the room. His eyes were hidden in shadow, but occasionally they seemed to flash with light as the torches brightened his countenance. His skin also seemed to glow, thought Cathryn, as though the light was drawn to it. Once he looked up and caught her watching him, and he held her gaze as they moved to the music on opposite ends of the hall. Perhaps it was the excitement of the dance, or maybe

29

the wine, but as his eyes rested on her, they seemed to shine more brightly, and Cathryn felt for a moment that the rest of the hall had faded, and that it was just the two of them. The feeling vanished in a moment as she was jostled and pulled, and when she looked back at him, he was laughing as his feet tangled with the girl beside him. He looked up again after that, but Cathryn quickly looked away, reality once more having asserted itself.

It was late by the time the musicians finally put away their instruments, pleading exhaustion. An elderly man, who had been quietly sitting on a bench at the side of the hall, now rose to his feet and slowly wound his way through the crowds to the front of the room. The man looked like he was unused to a roof over his head and a soft mattress — his grey hair, pulled into a rough queue, was unkempt and his hands were callused, while his weather-beaten face bespoke a man who spent most of his days sleeping under the stars. As he walked, the crowds parted before him, a ripple of chatter running through the crowd.

"It's the bard," Cathryn heard someone whisper. As the man made his way towards the dais, the noise grew louder as people began to shout their encouragements.

"Make it a good one, old man!" someone shouted.

"Nothing too gloomy," shouted another.

"I will tell the tale the good Lord gives me," responded the old man piously, before adding with a grin, "but first, ale! My throat is parched."

A cup of ale quickly found its way into the man's hands, and tipping back his head, he gulped it down in one long swallow. "More," he said hoarsely, wiping his sleeve across his mouth and holding out the cup. It was quickly filled to the brim once more, and this time he drank it down slowly.

"Ah! Much better," he said, his voice strong and steady when the second cup had been drained dry. He placed it on the table while it was replenished. "Now, let's see. What story is the good Lord giving me this night?" He grinned slyly and winked at his audience. Benches were being pulled away from the walls, pushed into a rough circle around the old man, as the crowd settled themselves more comfortably. Cathryn found herself on a bench next to old Master Kendrick, and he patted her hand gently as they waited.

"Good way to end an evening, eh my dear? With a tale from the past? All you young'uns need a chance to recover your breath. Too much strenuous activity just before sleep is detrimental to your health."

Cathryn smiled at the old man beside her, nodding her response before turning back towards the storyteller. She watched as he settled himself into a chair, pulling it around to the front of the dais, and she smiled in amusement as he drew out the process of shifting himself on the seat.

"Come on, old man," someone shouted, growing impatient. The bard bent a narrowed eye on the shouter before continuing with his preparations. Cathryn felt Master Kendrick shift beside her on the bench before getting up and moving away. She glanced up at his retreating figure, but in another moment someone else was sliding into his vacated space. The warmth that surrounded her gave Cathryn a clue as to who it was before she even glanced up at the face, her heart speeding up as Favian Drake looked down at her in amusement.

"Hoping for someone else, were you?" he said. "For someone who has absolutely no interest in me whatsoever, you have gone to great lengths to avoid me this evening."

Cathryn remembered her words to Peggy, and it was with this thought in mind that the question tumbled out. "Who says I have no interest in you?"

No sooner were the words out of her mouth than Cathryn was wishing them back, but it was too late. She looked away as Favian pounced.

"So you are interested in me?"

"Definitely not!"

"What a pity!" Favian said lightly. "It was wishful

thinking on my part, since I did hear you say most emphatically that you were not interested in me. Trying to convince yourself, were you?"

"How do you know that's what I said?" she asked carefully, keeping her eyes on the hands in her lap.

"You were practically shouting it at me, my dear, when you were telling Peggy that she was welcome to my attentions."

"I was not shouting," she hissed. "And I am not 'your dear'."

"I have extremely good hearing," he said. "It was as though you were calling to me across the room. And," he added, "you are most certainly dear to me."

Cathryn looked away in dismay and was relieved to see that the bard had finally settled himself on his seat, and was holding up his hand to begin.

"Urgh. Ahem." There were a few groans from the audience as he took his time clearing his throat before finally beginning. "Long, long ago, when the earth was still young," he started, his voice low and melodic, "people and animals lived together in peace, conversing with one another and sharing the land. But there was one creature who did not live in peace. One animal who desired, above all else, power over people and other animals. This beast lived to terrorize the people, and would devour them whole. The creature was especially fond of fair maidens, and would take its time savoring the young and tender flesh of a beautiful maid. Often, the maid was still alive as the monster ripped her apart from limb to limb, his burning breath blackening her flesh as people hid in anguish, unable to save her from her terrible torment as her screams for help went unanswered." The hall was silent as the audience listened with rapt attention. Next to her, Cathryn felt Favian tense, and she looked at him in surprise. He was watching the storyteller intently, his eyes narrowed, but at Cathryn's movement he glanced down at her, his expression softening.

"What's wrong," she whispered, "too much information for your sensibilities?" His mouth quirked for a moment before he bent his head closer to hers.

"I'm not very fond of dragon stories," he replied softly. "I find storytellers like to embellish far too much."

"Isn't that the point of a story?" she asked, her voice just as soft. Favian looked at her for a moment, before shrugging. "I suppose you are right," he said. Cathryn returned her attention to the storyteller as the man continued his tale.

"You all know that I speak of the dragon, the most dreadful of all the beasts that ever walked this earth." The words rolled from his mouth as he shook his fist in the air. "A creature so monstrous, so hideous, so terrible, that hell itself shook in terror." The man glanced around, his eyes wide, before he dropped his voice to just above a whisper. "A monster so evil, that there seemed none who could thwart it. A creature, it is said, that can take on the form of man, luring his unsuspecting victims to their deaths." The man lifted the cup in his hand to his lips and Cathryn could see his throat working as he swallowed another mouthful. Once again, he dragged his sleeve across his mouth before continuing. "But there was one, a knight so pure and good, brave, strong and courageous, he had the power to defeat the evil dragon." Cathryn glanced at Favian in amusement as she leaned towards him.

"Are you the good knight, Sir Drake?" she asked. He returned her look with a wry smile.

"Perhaps I'm the dragon." At his words, Cathryn snorted out a laugh, quickly covering her mouth with her hand when she saw others glancing at her in irritation. She sneaked a guilty look at Favian, and he lifted his eyebrows at her. She smiled back before returning her gaze to the old man. Beside her, Cathryn felt Favian shift in his seat, the movement bringing him slightly closer. Even though he did not touch her, she could feel the heat of him running down the length of her, as soft and gentle as an intimate caress. She felt her heart speed up again, each beat sounding like a drum pounding in her ears, and the thought flashed through her mind that if he could hear her whisper across a room, perhaps he could also hear her heartbeat. She glanced up at him to see him watching her intently. If he heard the thrumming in her chest, he gave no indication of it, but instead gazed at her, his eyes holding hers, the strange light that she sometimes saw burning a little brighter. Her lips parted slightly as she drew in a breath, and he glanced down at them for a moment, before looking in her eyes once again.

Leaning closer, he brought his lips close as he whispered in her ear. "Can I call on you sometime?"

Mutely, she nodded, an incline of the head so slight she wasn't even sure she had made the movement, but it was enough for him. He pulled back, accepting the response with his own slight nod, before turning around and sliding off the bench. He was gone a moment later, the warmth of his body quickly replaced by a cool breeze that stirred with the opening of the door as he exited.

Cathryn returned her attention to the storyteller, but her mind was distracted. It was with only half an ear that she heard the tale of the brave knight who had defeated the world's most wicked monster, piercing his heart with a double-edged sword, and finally avenging the lives of so many maidens who had been ripped to shreds by the terrible beast. But instead of a dragon, her mind was filled with thoughts of Favian. The man seemed determined to torment her, and now she had agreed, while caught up in a moment of insanity, to his request to call upon her. She would have to see him, of course, and use the opportunity to let him know that he was to leave her alone. But faced with the distraction of his presence, she wasn't sure she would even be able to. And therein lay the problem.

The tale of the defeated dragon brought the evening to a close, and it was not long after the story was done that people started to drift away, returning to their own homes either by foot or carriage. Father soon appeared at Cathryn's side, ready to attend her home.

"Did you enjoy your evening?" Father asked as they strolled along the street together, her arm tucked securely in his. The street was quiet, with not another soul around, and only a very faint glow emitting from the street lamps. The moon that had been shining so brightly earlier was now hidden by a blanket of cloud.

"I did, Father. And what about you?"

"Thomas and I were able to discuss our delegation to the king, so from that point it was certainly beneficial. The story was what you would expect from any traveling bard who would rather delve into tales of fairies and dragons instead of imparting knowledge of our glorious history. Still, it was entertaining. I am sure we were all relieved that the knight was victorious over such a monstrous beast."

"The knight was certainly very heroic. But I rather wish the dragon had not been quite so vicious."

"Oh well, you cannot make a monster be nice."

They walked in silence for a few minutes, until a hoot and a sudden flurry of wings broke the quiet. A moment later the owl swooped over them, barely missing their heads, and Cathryn looked around in alarm, feeling the hair at the back of her neck rise.

"What's that?" she whispered, gripping her father's arm in sudden fear. Father glanced around quickly before patting her arm.

"Nothing." He paused to clear his throat. "Nothing but your imagination playing tricks on you."

Cathryn wasn't so sure. She glanced around, pressing herself close to her father's side, but all was dark. The air was still and all was quiet, so quiet she could have heard a mouse scurrying across the road, but nothing stirred. She glanced around again, her body tense, and this time she saw a faint glimmer of gold shining through the darkness. The light seemed to be watching her, and she stared at it until it blinked back into darkness; and when, a moment later, the air in the lane stirred, she felt a rush of heat surround her and then disappear. As though the night had been holding its breath, its sounds suddenly resumed.

"Come," Father said, gently tugging her arm, "we should not tarry in these dark lanes."

Their house was around the next corner, and in another few minutes Father pushed open the door and Cathryn stepped through the doorway into the brightly-lit room beyond.

CHAPTER SEVEN

Cathryn was out of bed soon after the sun rose the following morning. She had had an unsettled night, pursued by dragons and eyes of burning gold. Quickly donning a riding habit, she slipped out of the house and walked down the road, covering the short distance that led to the town stables where her father kept their horses. A stable hand was asleep on a mound of straw in a corner near the entrance, but he scrambled to his feet at the sound of her approach, rubbing sleep from a pair of bleary eyes. Bits of straw clung to his hair, and Cathryn resisted the urge to pull them out, instead digging into her purse to find a few coins to toss to him in thanks. Despite his rude awakening, he quickly had Morana saddled, and a few minutes later, Cathryn was leaving the streets of the town behind her as she headed into the countryside, making for the large meadow that lay to the east of the town.

As the sun began to climb in the eastern sky, Cathryn urged the horse into a canter. The wind caught her hair and lifted it up from her neck as she leaned into the rhythm of her mount. There was an enormous oak tree at the far end of the meadow, and she raced towards it, hair whipping around her face. Her mind returned to the previous evening. The music and dancing had been most enjoyable, and the story had been entertaining. There was only one aspect that she tried to avoid thinking about, but thoughts of Favian Drake kept on intruding, just like the man himself. She had to admit, as much as it irked her to do so, that when she was in his presence all sense flew from her mind. Why else would she have agreed to his calling upon her?

The sun was high in the sky by the time Cathryn returned to the house. She was ascending the stairs when she heard Hannah behind her.

"Mistress Peggy is awaiting your presence in the parlor." She took Cathryn by the arm and dragged her up the stairs. "Let's get you out of that habit and make you presentable."

Under Hannah's ministrations, Cathryn was soon descending the stairs suitably attired. She crossed the hall and entered the parlor, watching Peggy in amusement as she jumped to her feet.

"Cathryn! Where have you been? I've been waiting for an eternity. I was just about to leave you a note and return another time."

"I was out riding," Cathryn said. "What are you doing up so early?"

"It was crucial that I see you. I think you've been hiding something regarding your relationship with Favian Drake."

"Hiding something? Relationship?" exclaimed Cathryn. "Whatever do you mean? As I said before, I have absolutely no interest in the man. Moreover, he spent the evening with you, not me."

"He may have spent the evening with me, but he could not stop asking me about you! He wanted to know how long I have known you. And how long you have known Geoffrey. Whether you had set a date for the exchange of vows. How old you were when your mother died." Peggy flung her hands into the air with each question, her tone growing more accusatory with each one.

"Stop!" Cathryn held up one hand as she placed the other over her forehead. "Whatever his reason for asking these questions, there is nothing between us. I barely even know the man. And furthermore, as you know, I am promised to Geoffrey."

"What does that have to do with it?" Peggy said in surprise. "We all know that is a business arrangement. Follow your heart, Cathryn, but just be discreet."

"No! I would never do that!"

"Why not? Geoffrey does," Peggy said with a shrug. Cathryn dropped her hand and stared at her friend. The news didn't really surprise her, but hearing it said aloud was still somewhat distressing. For a brief moment she wondered how it was Peggy knew this about Geoffrey, but she shook off the thought. She wasn't sure she really wanted to know the answer. And what Geoffrey did was no concern of hers, she reminded herself, as long as it didn't interfere with their business arrangement.

"I would not do it," she answered slowly, "because *I* believe in the sanctity of the marriage vow. And furthermore, it would not be fair to either myself or the other person to allow ourselves to be involved in something that could never be permanent."

"Perhaps the other person does not want anything permanent," Peggy suggested.

"Then he would just be using me," Cathryn said, "and I would not want to be entangled with someone like that." She stood up and walked around the room, before facing her friend once more. "This is a pointless discussion, since I am not in the slightest bit interested in Favian Drake."

"Really?" said Peggy.

"Really. I just wish he would leave me alone! And even if I did have feelings for him," she added, "I still wouldn't want to have anything to do with him, since I have seen how following your heart only leads you into a morass of misery."

"What a cynic you are," said Peggy with a laugh. "I won't say any more, but I do think you are deluding yourself. I think that you are far more interested than you will admit. But enough of that," she said as Cathryn opened her mouth to protest, "Did you hear the news about Mary Walsh?"

CHAPTER EIGHT

The weeks following the Bradshaw party were mild and warm, giving Cathryn hope that she could soon start her tour of the wool estates. She spent the days reviewing contracts with suppliers, analyzing wool prices, and examining the latest trends in cloth sales. She also spent time with Felix plotting the route she would take with her entourage, and oversaw the planning of the supplies that would be necessary for six weeks on the road. In addition to Felix, she would also be accompanied by Hannah and a dozen wagoners and wagons.

The days slipped by, and Favian did not come to call. Cathryn pushed away the disappointment she felt, trying to convince herself that she was relieved. After all, what man asked if he could call and then did not come?

But when Hannah knocked on her door one morning and informed her that a gentleman was awaiting her in the parlor, she could not help smiling. She smoothed down her gown, pushed her hairpin more securely in place, and made her way down the stairs. She paused at the threshold, taking in the sight of Favian as he slowly turned to face her.

"Mistress Cathryn," he said with a bow. Cathryn stepped

into the room, inclining her head in acknowledgement.

"Master Drake," she responded.

"My apologies for not calling on you sooner," he said, "but something came up that needed my attention."

Cathryn sank down into a chair and gestured for him to take a seat on the other side of the room.

"No need to concern yourself, Master Drake," she said. "I had quite forgotten that you had intended to call." She dropped her eyes to her lap as she spoke. Favian eyed her narrowly for a moment before nodding.

"In that case I won't trouble you any further, Mistress," he said. "Please forgive the intrusion." Cathryn bit her lip as he stood up, determined not to delay his leaving. This was, after all, what she wanted. But as he got to the door, he turned back to her once more.

"Tell me, Cathryn," he said, "ten years hence, when you are staring at a husband for whom you feel nothing but contempt, will you still feel that passing up the chance of love was the right choice?"

Cathryn rose to her feet, stung. "How dare you?" she demanded. "What makes you think I will feel contempt for my husband?"

"You will," he said.

"What are you suggesting? That I will find love with you?"

"You will never know now, will you?"

"You are quite out of line," she said. "This is no way for a gentleman to act."

"I never said I was a gentleman, Cathryn. But whatever I am, we both know that you have feelings for me."

"You are so … so arrogant," she fumed. "And I most certainly do not have feelings for you." She turned around, presenting her back to him. He stepped up behind her, and she could feel the warmth of his presence.

"Do you not, Cathryn?" he said softly. "Because I most certainly have feelings for you."

She shivered slightly at his words, determined not to look around at him, but when he took her by the shoulders and turned her around, she was unable to resist. Bending down, he caught her lips with his, and she opened her mouth in response as his warm breath swept over her. All rational thought flew from her mind as she felt her body respond to his touch. His hands slipped around to her back, pulling her closer, and she leaned into him, lifting her hands to touch him. The lapse was momentary, and she pulled away, aghast at her reaction. Placing her hands on his chest she pushed him away, but before she removed them, he caught them in his own and held them captured.

"Let me go," she whispered.

"Not until you admit you have feelings for me," he said.

"No! No!" Cathryn twisted herself loose and turned away, dropping her head into her hands. She drew in a deep breath before lifting her face to stare out the window.

"No," she repeated. "It doesn't matter whether or not I have feelings for you. I am betrothed to another of my own free will, and I will not dishonor that commitment."

"Ah, yes, that business arrangement," said Favian dryly. "Tell me, Cathryn, will that business arrangement keep you warm at night when your husband is out whoring with other women? Will it bring you comfort when he spends the night over drinks with friends instead of with you? Will it bring you contentment in your old age when you sit at a fire alone, with only dry numbers to keep you company? Because that is what your future holds."

Cathryn winced as Favian flung out each question. She turned around slowly, desperately trying to find an adequate reply, but she was alone in the room, the door already swinging closed. Dropping down to her knees, she sunk onto the floor, allowing the tears she had been holding back to fall onto the cold stone floor.

CHAPTER NINE

The only thing still preventing Cathryn from starting her tour was the unsettled spring weather. Traveling with a convoy of wagons and other equipage over rough country lanes was hazardous even when the weather was fine, so traveling when the lanes were still mired down in mud was a foolish risk. And faced with the certainty that there would be times they would have to camp under the stars, Cathryn was prepared to wait for more clement weather. But the wait was trying, and even Father could see that she was growing short-tempered.

"I think we are nearing the end of the wet weather," Father assured her one clear morning. "I'm sure things will have settled in the next week or two." Cathryn clamped her teeth together in frustration, glancing out the window as she did so. Through the open shutters she could hear the sounds of the market — a riotous racket where it seemed like all manner of life were competing against each other to make themselves heard — roosters, geese, lambs and pigs lamenting their sorry plights as merchants and sellers yelled out the natures of their wares. Making a quick decision, she gave her father a smile before slipping out the door of his study. Pausing only to fetch her purse and swing a cloak around her shoulders, she made her way out onto the street, following the din to the market.

Once there, Cathryn meandered through the tightly packed stalls of merchandise, twisting adroitly to avoid being knocked over by carefree children and determined shoppers. She paused at a merchant who had a table of polished stones. There was one that caught her eye — a clear, translucent disc of dark orange.

"That would be amber, Mistress," said the merchant, observing her interest. "Brought from far distant lands, traversing hundreds of miles. It can be yours for ten silver coins."

"Ten silver coins? That's too dear for me," Cathryn said.

"Ah, but for you Mistress, I will sell it for only eight silver coins. That is a bargain you will not see again."

"You are too kind, Master," she said. "But I'm afraid I must decline." She laid the stone down on the table, smiling to herself when the man spoke again.

"Did I say eight coins, Mistress? I meant seven, yours for only seven."

"Hmm, only seven?" She lifted the amber once more, prepared to examine it more closely, when a voice sounded softly in her ear behind her.

"Cathryn?"

For just an instant, Cathryn felt the sun stand still in its travels through the heavens as her heart started to pound. Carefully replacing the disc on the cloth, she turned around to face the man who would not give her peace.

"Master Drake," she said, with a very slight nod. "We meet again."

"Yes." He stared down at her for a moment, his eyes searching her face, before turning his shoulder and gesturing to a woman standing behind him. She was tall, only a few inches shorter than Favian, and Cathryn guessed her to be in her early forties. And although her coloring was dark, she had the same sapphire-blue eyes as Favian.

"Mistress Cathryn, I would like to introduce my mother, Margaret Drake."

"Madame Drake," Cathryn said, quickly adjusting her mental musings on the woman's age as she dropped a shallow curtsey.

The woman smiled, reaching out to take Cathryn's hand in her own.

"It is a pleasure to meet you, my dear. Please, call me Margaret. And may I call you Cathryn?" She glanced over at her son. "It is how Favian refers to you, so I have become quite used to it in my mind."

"Yes, of course," Cathryn said. She also glanced at Favian, wondering what he had said about her, but his expression was closed.

"You can come find us in half an hour," Margaret said to Favian. "Cathryn and I are going to spend some time getting acquainted." Favian looked taken aback at being so summarily dismissed, but he took it with good humor.

"Make sure you inform Cathryn of all my charming qualities," he teased, before turning and heading away.

Margaret watched his retreating figure for a moment before turning to look at the amber still lying on the cloth. The merchant, who had discreetly moved away when Favian and Margaret joined Cathryn, now moved back towards the two women. Picking up the piece of amber, Margaret turned it over in her hands.

"This is a pretty piece," she said. "I bought one only slightly larger at another market recently, and paid five silver coins for it." The merchant shot Margaret a glare as she smiled blandly back at him, before turning to Cathryn in defeat.

"Five silver coins, then," he said.

"Four," said Margaret. "As I said, my piece was larger." The man shook his head with a look of infinite despair.

"Very well, four," he said. "Highway robbery, it is, with

me having seven mouths to feed. The children will go to bed with empty stomachs tonight." He shook his head sadly as Cathryn handed him the coins.

"Only seven children," replied Margaret with a deepening smile. "I was certain it was nine, but perhaps I have you confused with someone else." A flush rose in the merchant's cheeks, but he held Margaret's gaze.

"Must'ave been someone else, Mistress," he said. "Good day to you."

"I will hazard a guess that that was the same merchant you dealt with before," Cathryn said with a grin as they moved away.

"Yes, it most certainly was. Audacious fellow. I know for a fact that his *three* children are all grown, with children of their own, and his wife does not suffer from a dearth of sustenance." Margaret glanced at Cathryn as she spoke. "He lives in the city close to our estate, so he is well known to me."

"The city close to your estate? Where exactly is your estate?"

"It lies thirty-five miles to the north."

"Thirty-five miles? That's more than two hours' ride away. Do you have a house in town as well?"

"No, but I am visiting a friend for a few days. Perhaps you know her? Madame Bradshaw?"

"Yes, I certainly do know Madame Bradshaw. Her husband has business dealings with my father." Cathryn paused for a moment before returning to her previous confusion. "But Favian must have a house here. He seems to be frequently in town." She was startled to realize that she didn't know a great deal about Favian.

"No, I believe he covers the distance from our home and back each time. He has a swift mount, and is happy to traverse the distance," Margaret replied. "Perhaps," she added softly, "he feels it is worth the effort."

Cathryn looked away as she felt the blush mounting in

her cheeks, but it quickly faded as Margaret directed her attention to a display of finely woven fabrics, dyed in rich shades of color.

"Look at these lovely hues," she exclaimed. "This yellow would look very becoming on you," she said, holding the cloth up to Cathryn's face. She spent a few more moments admiring the weave and colors, before strolling towards the next table, on which was displayed a collection of hairpins.

"Now this," Cathryn said, picking up one of the pieces, "is something I am always losing. I will purchase another one now and make my maid very happy." She dug out a few small coins and handed them over as Margaret waited by her side. As they continued to stroll through the market, Margaret turned to look at her.

"I will be returning home in two days, but if you have some time available, please call on me before I leave. Favian speaks very admiringly of you, and I would like to further our acquaintance while the opportunity exists. Madame Bradshaw is a very late riser, so I am free in the mornings. Can I expect you to call tomorrow?"

Cathryn hesitated before answering. She liked this friendly and unpretentious woman, and wanted to get to know her more, but she did not want Margaret to believe that she returned Favian's regard for her.

"Yes, I would like that," Cathryn said cautiously, "but I don't want to visit under false pretenses. I am betrothed to another man."

"Yes, I am aware of your longstanding commitment," Margaret said, "Regardless of your situation, I would still like to further our acquaintance." Margaret smiled and patted her hand, before turning away and scanning the marketplace.

"Favian is probably wondering where we have gotten to. Ah, there he is now." Cathryn glanced in the same direction as Margaret, and was rewarded with the sight of Favian scanning the crowds with narrowed eyes. A moment later he saw them, and turning in their direction, quickly closed the distance.

"I was beginning to wonder whether I would ever find you again in this crowd," Favian said to his mother.

"I have no fear of that," responded his parent. Turning to Cathryn, she added, "He has the eyes of a hawk."

Cathryn turned to look at Favian with eyebrows raised.

"Eyes of a hawk and ears of a bat. You are a man of startling abilities, Master Drake. Do you have the nose of a bloodhound too?"

Favian flashed a quick frown at his mother, composing his features into a bland expression as he returned his gaze to Cathryn.

"Perhaps I do. Should we test it out on you?" He took a step towards her, and grinned when she hurriedly stepped back. "You know," he said with a slight smirk, "if my mother wasn't here I would tell you that I already know your scent is like that of the early morning air laden with dew, with a hint of roses, but I would not wish to embarrass her."

Margaret coughed beside her, and Cathryn glared at Favian, suppressing a sharp retort.

"It would appear you have failed in your intention, Master Drake," she said, glaring at him. Turning to Margaret, she dropped a small curtsey. "Madame Drake, I will see you tomorrow."

CHAPTER TEN

Cathryn paused on her way to the Bradshaws' the following morning, glancing around the street. In the daylight it looked quite benign, but it was here, under cover of darkness, that she had seen strange glowing lights, heard eerie silences and felt suspicious breezes. There was nothing threatening now, and after a moment she carried on walking in the direction of the Bradshaws'.

Margaret was seated in the back parlor when Cathryn arrived, and rising, took Cathryn by the hands and led her to a seat beside her own.

"Make yourself comfortable, my dear. I am so delighted you were able to call upon me this morning, since I leave at first light tomorrow," Margaret said.

"Do you travel alone?" Cathryn asked.

"Oh, no. My husband is coming into town to fetch me." She sighed with a smile. "I am always happy to return home since I miss my garden when I am away. Each day there is something new to see, and at the moment it is coming into full bloom."

"That sounds lovely," Cathryn said wistfully. "I have lived my whole life in town, but have always imagined what it would be like to have private gardens to wander in. Does your estate include woods?"

"Yes, there are woods to the east of the house, which will be purple with bluebells, and beyond the gardens there is wilderness, where wildflowers grow in profusion. At the moment it will be full of wild daffodils and crocuses." Margaret watched Cathryn closely as she spoke, before rising and offering her a glass of wine from a pitcher on the table. "I understand from Master Bradshaw that you will be going on the road for your father's wool business," said Margaret, as she returned to her seat.

"Yes," Cathryn said. "I'm hoping that the weather will allow me to set out before the end of the month."

"You are quite active in this business, I understand," Margaret said. "Have you done a tour before?"

"Never without Father, but Father's bailiff will travel with me."

"Well, Master Bradshaw considers you very competent, which is high praise indeed, and your father evidently considers you worthy of his trust. Are you an only child?"

"Yes, my mother died in childbirth when I was very young," replied Cathryn.

"And your father never remarried."

"No, he always said his work was a far more consistent lover."

"You must have had a lonely childhood."

"I never felt the want of company," Cathryn said. "As a child I managed to keep myself amused, and as I grew older, my father spent time teaching me the business."

"Well, I think Favian would envy you the lack of siblings. He has an older sister, with whom he was always at odds. Of course, he seemed particularly well versed at being an annoying younger brother, and for every slight he suffered at his sister's hands, he gave back twice as much. His father was always trying to keep him under control, but he would just as soon discover some new source of mischief. He splashed the juice of blackberries into Ayleth's hair once while she slept, and for weeks she had purple streaks in her hair." Margaret laughed at the memory. "Ayleth never forgot it either, and years later, she poured honey on his, er, in his hair while he slept. It created a dreadful mess, but Favian is far more forgiving than his sister." Margaret took a sip of her wine. "You must have had a governess as you were growing up?"

"No. My father believed an education in the warehouse would be of more value than learning needlework and music from a governess."

"And you don't regret the lack of learning in these areas?"

"I don't suppose I have given it a lot of thought. I used to wish I could learn to play the lute, but my father did allow me to indulge my passion for books to a certain degree."

As the hours slid by, Margaret listened as Cathryn spoke more about her childhood, the education she had received from her father, and how her betrothal had come about. Margaret, in turn, shared with Cathryn her passion for horticulture and herbals. As the lady of a large manor, she was often called upon to administer physics and tonics to the villeins who lived on their estate, and Cathryn listened in delight as she told stories about some of the people she had helped. It was already past noon when Cathryn rose and regretfully said her farewells, expressing her regret at the distance of Margaret's estate from the town.

"I would love to further our acquaintance," she said, "and also see your garden."

"Perhaps you will," was Margaret's reply.

CHAPTER ELEVEN

Cathryn was seated in her father's study two days later when the note arrived. It was from Margaret, inviting her to spend a few nights with her at her home in the country.

'In addition to the enjoyment of your company,' read the note, 'I would love to share the delights of my garden, which is looking quite lovely, with such an enthusiastic admirer. If you are agreeable, I will send the carriage for you on Monday morning, and will return you home again Wednesday afternoon.'

"Who is your note from?" Father asked, watching his daughter with interest.

"It's from Madame Drake. She has invited me to visit her at her home in the country." She looked at her father with a smile of eagerness.

"Of course you should go," Father said. "Has she mentioned dates?" Cathryn read him the note, but then the smile dropped from her face.

"Actually, I don't think I will go."

"Why ever not? You seemed quite taken with the idea a moment ago."

"There is still much to be done to get ready for the

tour."

"Nonsense. You have done nothing but prepare for the tour for the last two weeks. You need to spend time with your friends as well, and it is only for two nights."

"But —"

"And furthermore, you have been poor company of late. You need a distraction while you wait for the weather to improve."

"But —"

"Cathryn, is there anything in the lady's character that is making you hesitate?"

"No."

"Then I insist you go." Cathryn twisted her hands in her lap. She had no wish to reveal that the true reason for her reluctance to go was the possibility of Favian's presence at Drake Manor.

"Very well, Father. I will notify Madame Drake of my acceptance."

"Good. And you will see that I am right. I predict you will return quite refreshed."

Cathryn was ready when the carriage arrived promptly at nine o'clock on Monday morning. Hannah stood at the door, pouting at being left behind, although Cathryn had told her to take the days off. Her valise had been stowed when her father handed her into the carriage, and she sank into the plush seating before pulling back the curtain that hung over the small window. Father was standing on the step, waiting to wave goodbye as the carriage pulled away.

It was almost noon by the time the carriage swept up a long driveway to stop in front of a large, stone house with high crenellated walls, from behind which peeked a steeply pitched roof of wood. On either end of the house jutted multi-sided towers, while a square entrance porch, with roses climbing over the yellow stone walls, stood towards the right end of the long building. It was from here that Margaret Drake emerged, a tall man striding out close behind her. He cut a striking figure, and with his blazing red hair, Cathryn guessed that he must be Favian's father. This was soon confirmed when Margaret introduced him to her guest.

"Welcome to Drake Manor." She greeted Cathryn with a smile. "Allow me to introduce my husband, Owain."

"Master Drake," greeted Cathryn with a curtsey.

"You are most welcome, Mistress," Owain responded. "My wife is surrounded by men who can be less than refined, so it is good for her to enjoy some more feminine company for a change." He cast a mischievous smile at his wife as she moved forward to clasp Cathryn's hands.

"Come, my dear, you must be weary. Let me show you to your room where you can refresh yourself."

Brushing past her husband with a smile, Margaret led Cathryn through the porch into the hall. The large room reached the full height of the building, with a timbered roof that rose from the walls at a steep pitch that matched the roof she had seen outside. Long, multi-paned windows ran along the length of the walls, filling the room with light. At the far end of the hall was a raised dais, with a wooden screen behind, while at both ends of the hall arched doorways led to passages beyond. It was through the closest doorway that Margaret led Cathryn. Three more doors led from the passage, and Margaret paused at the first.

"This is the small parlor, where I will await you." She continued down the passage, pointing out the small dining room and library, Cathryn close at her heels. Half way along the passage the wall to the left became a half wall, interspersed with pillars, over which the courtyard could be seen. Cathryn could see doorways where the hall opened into the courtyard, which bustled with activity, while on the opposite side another wing of the building also faced the courtyard, leaving just one side of the courtyard open. Cathryn paused to take in the scene, while Margaret glanced over her shoulder.

"The kitchen, pantry and buttery occupy that side of the building," she explained. "And upstairs are chambers, one of which is currently used by our nephew."

At the end of the passage was a steep, spiral staircase, and Cathryn followed Margaret towards it.

"Your nephew resides with you?" she asked as they mounted the stairs.

"Well," Margaret paused in her ascent, turning to look at Cathryn as she answered. "'Resides' is not strictly accurate. Aaron comes and goes as he pleases, and never spends more than a night or two at a time. He can be quite ... unsocial, and as he knows of your visit, I do not expect to see him for the duration of your stay." She turned and continued up the stairs as Cathryn absorbed this, stepping out onto another passage. There was a door to the left, through which Margaret led Cathryn.

"Your chambers while you are here, my dear," Margaret said, her hand sweeping over the room. Directly opposite the doorway a window was set into the thick walls, and Cathryn crossed the room to view the aspect. The house sat on a slight rise, and from this section of the house stretched green lawns that rolled away down a gentle slope towards woods that stood in the distance.

"It is lovely, thank you."

"Take your time refreshing yourself, and I will meet you in the parlor when you are ready," Margaret said as she left the room, pulling the door closed behind her.

Cathryn looked around the room, noting that her valise already sat at the foot of the canopied bed. The bed drapes had been tied back, and Cathryn could see the fine embroidered coverlet that lay atop the mattress. To the right of the window ran a long table, on which sat a basin and ewer, already filled with water, and a pitcher of wine, with a crystal glass resting beside it. Despite the milder temperatures of the day, a fire roared in the hearth across from the bed.

Pulling her cloak off her shoulders, Cathryn threw it onto a stool and crossed to the table, where she poured herself a glass of wine. A stack of linens lay beside the basin, and within a short time she felt herself ready to head back downstairs.

The parlor that Cathryn stepped into was at the front of the house, in one of the multi-sided towers Cathryn had seen from outside. Windows were set in the angled walls, allowing for views of the front, side and back of the house, making the whole room seem alive as light danced through the uneven windowpanes. Margaret had been plying a needle as Cathryn entered the room, but she set the embroidery aside as she looked up at the younger woman.

"Help yourself to something to eat," said Margaret, gesturing to a tray of bread and cold meat that lay on a small table near the window. "I thought we could tour the gardens this afternoon, if that arrangement suits you." Cathryn agreed this was a wonderful plan, and after nibbling on a few morsels, indicated herself ready to start.

CHAPTER TWELVE

The afternoon passed quickly as Cathryn followed Margaret around the gardens at Drake Manor. They had been laid out in a rectangular plan, at the center of which was a large circular pond. The surface of the water was littered with the broad leaves of water lilies, and as Cathryn drew near, she heard the plop of frogs as they jumped beneath the surface, joining the fish that moved lazily though the water. Around the pond was a gravel path, and beyond the path was grass, broken into four sections by paths that radiated outward. In each section of grass was a raised bed, bordered by lavender, where various herbs and flowers grew, while in each corner stood a lemon tree, the blossoms scenting the warm air. The whole was bordered by a high hedge, beyond which lay another walkway, over which grew trellised vines creating a covered passage, where benches of marble and hidden nooks could be found. It was the perfect place to while away the hours in quiet contemplation or engaging conversation, and the time slipped by as Margaret shared her memories of Drake Manor with Cathryn.

It was growing late by the time Cathryn and Margaret emerged from the gardens. When Cathryn indicated her disappointment that she hadn't seen the woods or wilderness beyond, Margaret was quick to reassure her.

"We still have the whole of tomorrow," she said. "Perhaps you would enjoy exploring on horseback?"

"Yes, that would be lovely."

"You enjoy riding?"

"Very much so. I have a beautiful mare that I try and ride as often as I can. There is an open meadow just beyond the town gate, and it is the one place where I feel completely free. At the far end is an enormous oak tree, and Morana and I ride as though the devil were on our heels." She laughed self-consciously as Margaret smiled.

"I enjoy riding as well. I will arrange for the horses to be saddled and ready in the morning."

The two women had reached the house, and passing under the porch, entered the hall. "I need to speak to the steward," said Margaret, "so I will take my leave of you for now. Supper will be ready soon, so join us in the dining room when you are ready. Except for Sundays and feast days, we prefer to take our meals there."

Thanking her hostess, Cathryn headed down the narrow passageway towards the spiral staircase. She glanced over the wall into the courtyard as she passed, pausing to watch the antics of some children playing at swords, when a slight movement above the scene caught her eye. Glancing up, she saw a man standing in the upper passageway, his arms crossed over his chest. He wore no tunic, leaving his muscled chest bare, and although he looked slighter than Favian, Cathryn saw no reason to doubt his strength. He had golden brown hair that hung over his shoulders, and from some trick of the light, his eyes seemed to be blazing. He was staring at her, his gaze lowered, direct, and angry. She drew back behind a pillar in fright, her heart pounding in her chest, before risking another look, but the man had gone. Leaning back against the pillar, she drew in a deep breath, wondering who the person could be. Checking once more that the man was gone, she ran up the stairs to her chambers, where she settled the bar across the door and crossed over to the pitcher of wine, pouring herself a glass with shaking hands.

By the time Cathryn had changed into a gown of sapphire blue, and had braided and coiled her hair, securing it with a pin of silver and bronze, the feeling of dread had passed. In fact, she was glad no-one had been around to see her foolish display. It seemed unlikely that the Drakes would be harboring any dangerous criminals, and even if the person was not pleasant, as a guest of the Drakes he would do nothing to threaten her. She made her way down the stairs to the dining room, where Margaret and Owain were already waiting.

"Have you recovered from your journey?" Owain asked Cathryn as they sat down.

"Yes, thank you. I spent a most pleasant afternoon in the gardens." She paused a moment. "I saw someone in the passage opposite mine earlier. Was that your nephew?" She watched as Owain and Margaret exchanged a quick look.

"What did he look like, my dear?" Margaret asked.

Cathryn blushed as she replied. "He had light brown hair, but his chest was bare. He appeared to be rather angry about something."

"That sounds like him. I dare say you caught him unawares, which is why he appeared angry."

"Yes, you are probably right." Cathryn nodded.

She turned her head at the sound of Favian walking into the room, his eyebrows drawn together in a frown. He gave her a quick glance as he walked around the table.

"Who is angry?" he asked, bending down to give his mother a kiss on the cheek.

"Aaron," said Owain. "Cathryn saw him earlier."

"Ah," said Favian, meeting and holding Owain's gaze.

It was loaded, that 'ah', thought Cathryn. Perhaps her fears hadn't been foolish after all. She looked down as

Favian switched his gaze to her.

"You are perfectly safe here," he said. He dropped down into a seat next to his mother, grabbing a shank of lamb off a platter and placing it on a plate.

"You haven't eaten?" his mother asked.

"I have," he said with a grin, "but I am a growing lad." He turned to face his father. "I was over at Morgan's earlier, helping him repair his roof." Owain nodded as Favian explained. "Morgan is one of our tenants, and his roof caught alight the other day. Thankfully the house was empty. It is uncertain how the fire started, but not too much damage was done."

"Perhaps it was lightning," Cathryn suggested.

"Well, that is a possibility," Favian said, "except that the sky was clear." There was a note of challenge in his voice that urged Cathryn to respond.

"Well, maybe an ember from the hearth."

"Hmm, the roof had been burnt from the outside, though," Favian said, smiling in amusement.

"Perhaps someone set it deliberately."

"Yes, but who would do that?"

"Favian ..." Owain said, but Favian ignored him.

"The man is liked well enough, and no-one saw anything suspicious," he said, placing his arms on the table and leaning towards her, his eyes intent.

"A villain, bent on havoc then."

"True, but I like to think that someone would have noticed a stranger lurking about."

"Well, I don't know," Cathryn said, exasperated. "Maybe it was a dragon!"

Favian leaned back in his seat and crossed his arms over his chest, his mouth twitching with laughter.

"Maybe it was, at that," he said.

"Just ignore him, my dear," said Margaret, glaring at her son. He glanced at her, unrepentant, before returning his gaze to Cathryn. She met the challenge for a moment, and then turned to Owain, a smile pasted on her face.

"Do you have many tenants?" she asked.

"A few," he replied, glancing at Favian, before settling his gaze on their guest. "Most of our land is given over to pasture though."

"Sheep?" said Cathryn, her interest piqued. Owain's smile widened.

"Yes, sheep," he said.

"Ah. What breed?"

"Lincolns."

"Oh, really?" Cathryn said, glancing up as a servant placed a tray of sweetmeats on the table. Lincolns were prized for their long wool, which produced very fine cloth. Owain watched her quietly as she made her selection from the tray.

"How many?" she asked, before popping a tiny fruit pastry into her mouth.

"Two thousand." Owain eyed the tray before leaning forward to make his own selection. Cathryn suppressed a smile. Two thousand was a good-sized flock.

"And what do you do with the wool?" she asked, quelling the urge to lick her fingers. The pastry was delicious.

"Some years we take it to market. Other years we negotiate a contract with a merchant," he said. "But it is Favian who deals with these matters."

"Oh," she said, casting Favian a quick glance. He was still leaning back in his seat, listening to the conversation without comment. He grinned at her evident dismay.

"I'm quite willing to discuss terms," he said, "but be warned that I hold to the maxim 'act in haste, repent at leisure,' so our negotiations may be fairly lengthy."

Cathryn ground her teeth in frustration. She was under no illusion as to what Favian was doing. Lengthy negotiations meant hours spent alone with the man. She did a quick calculation in her mind. Two thousand sheep would see a good return — not something to be lightly turned away from. She nodded, silently agreeing to his terms.

Margaret had been observing the conversation silently, but at Cathryn's acquiescence, she tapped her hand on the table.

"Enough business for one night. Come Cathryn, let us retire to the parlor." She nodded at the men. "Join us when you are ready."

CHAPTER THIRTEEN

Cathryn spent a pleasant few hours in the company of Margaret and Owain, ignoring Favian where he sat quietly observing her from a darkened corner. She stood as Margaret and Owain retired for the evening, determined to follow their example and head for her bed.

"Cathryn," Favian said, but Cathryn held up her hand to interrupt.

"Please, Favian, I'm very tired," she said.

"I want to propose a truce," he continued, ignoring her interruption. Cathryn looked at him in surprise.

"A truce?"

"Yes. You are here as my mother's guest, and I do not want you to feel uneasy. As long as you are staying here, we will treat each other with perfect respectability."

Cathryn eyed him suspiciously. "You won't say anything about my betrothal?"

"Only if you don't."

"And you won't discuss your feelings for me?"

"Not so long as you do not wish me to." Cathryn continued to look as he went on. "I will behave like a perfect gentleman. We can become better acquainted."

"Friends then?"

Favian smiled wryly. "We can try."

Cathryn nodded. She wasn't willing to lower her guard, but you don't look a gift horse in the mouth, she knew. Unsure how to continue, she watched him cautiously from across the room, but he took matters into his own hands.

"Do you read?"

"Of course. I learnt to read when I was still a child."

"Oh, I know that. What I meant was, do you read for enjoyment?"

"Whenever I am able. Unfortunately, Father believes that the only books worth reading are those that will impart knowledge and increase understanding, so there is little opportunity for me to read for pleasure."

"Well, we have a fine library here at Drake Manor, and you are welcome to borrow one or two titles. Would you like to see it?"

"Oh yes!" All thought of sleep flew from Cathryn's mind. "I would love to." Favian smiled.

"Come," he said, leading the way out the door and heading down the passage. He paused at a door and gestured for her to enter first, following close on her heels and almost bumping into her when she stopped in her tracks. The room was filled with more books than she had ever seen. Opposite the doorway was a window which looked out towards the front lawn, while on either side of the window was shelf upon shelf, all filled with leather-bound tomes. A fire burned in a grate set in the wall to the right, while a desk stood in the center of the room. Cathryn looked around, her eyes taking in the rows of books that lined the walls, before moving slowly forward. She headed to a shelf and ran her fingers over the embossed leather spines, reading the titles softly as she did so, before turning around to face Favian.

"This is incredible! Where did you get all these books?"

Favian shrugged. "My father's been collecting them for

many years."

"But there must be over a hundred!" Turning back to the shelf, Cathryn slowly moved along its length, reading the titles under her breath. She paused at *Canterbury Tales*, and reaching up, pulled the heavy volume off the shelf. The book had a thick leather cover, the title embossed in gold. Carrying the book over to the desk, Cathryn opened it carefully, turning the pages until she reached the Prologue. The writing was in a fine script, carefully executed by a master scribe, the first letter of each page beautifully decorated in bright hues. Curling tendrils embellished the margins of the yellowing pages, and Cathryn traced them with her finger, skimming through the opening lines of the tale. She gave Favian a sly look as she read aloud the description of the knight:

> *He found the highest favor in all eyes,*
> *A valiant warrior who was also wise*
> *And in deportment meek as any maid.*
> *He never spoke unkindly, never played*
> *The villain's part, but always did the right.*
> *He truly was a perfect, gentle knight.*

"Was it you that Chaucer saw at the Tabard, going on pilgrimage?" she asked.

Favian leaned over her shoulder as she read, and with a laugh, turned the page and read another passage:

> *Of table manners she had learnt it all,*
> *For from her lips she'd let no morsel fall*
> *Nor deeply in her sauce her fingers wet;*
> *She'd lift her food so well she'd never get*
> *A single drop or crumb upon her breast.*
> *At courtesy she really did her best.*

Cathryn tried to pull the book away, but in a movement

so fast she could not track it, Favian swung around to the other side of the table, taking the book with him. His voice was choked with laughter as he continued to read, moving away again as she quickly rounded the desk.

> *Her upper lip she wiped so very clean*
> *That not one bit of grease was ever seen*
> *Upon her drinking cup. She was discreet*
> *And never reached unseemly for the meat.*
> *And certainly she was good company,*
> *So pleasant and so amiable, while she*
> *Would in her mien take pains to imitate*
> *The ways of court, the dignity of state,*
> *That all might praise her for her worthiness.*

"You are so impertinent," she said, her voice filled with laughter. He looked at her over the desk as he finished reading, his blue eyes creased with laughter, but as their eyes met the laughter fell away, and the room fell into silence. She shivered, and he closed his eyes, breaking the spell.

"You're cold," he said. "Come stand next to the fire." The fire was behind him, and as he moved away, Cathryn walked around the desk to stand before the flames. A wayward strand of hair fell across her face, and she lifted a hand to push it away before smoothing it over the rest of her hair. The movement loosened the hairpin that was holding her hair in place, and she groaned as she felt the pin tumble from its knot, turning in time to see it spill into the flames.

Favian darted forward, his hand chasing the falling article into the fire as the blaze brushed his skin. He jerked his hand out again, empty, as Cathryn's groan of dismay turned to one of horror, and she caught his hand in her own, certain the burns would be severe. But although his skin was hot, it appeared to be untouched by the flames. Turning it over, Cathryn subjected the hand to a thorough examination, before looking up in confusion to meet Favian's sardonic gaze.

"I stand at risk of breaking my promise," he said, taking a step closer. Long fingers wrapped around hers before sliding up her hand in an intimate caress. Pulling herself free from his grasp, she stepped back, tripping over a pile of logs stacked next to the grate. Catching herself on the wall, she stepped clear of the fallen firewood as Favian watched, a slight frown creasing his forehead.

"I, uh, thought you had burnt yourself," said Cathryn awkwardly, "but I was mistaken."

"As you can see, I am quite unharmed," said Favian, looking away. "Was that pin of particular value to you?"

"No," replied Cathryn. "I have a proclivity for losing them, and that is the fifth in as many weeks. But the loss is not significant, and the item is not irreplaceable — it is merely the annoyance. I am glad you didn't injure yourself in your efforts to save it."

"Your concern for my well-being is much appreciated, Mistress," replied Favian. Cathryn looked down at the floor, refusing to meet his gaze.

"I will bid you goodnight," she said, turning towards the door.

"Goodnight, Cathryn," he said, executing an elegant bow. "I will see you on the morrow."

Cathryn nodded, sweeping past him and out into the passage. As she reached the stairway, she glanced back over her shoulder, catching Favian's gaze as he watched her from the doorway.

CHAPTER FOURTEEN

It rained during the night, a shower that tapped out a rhythmic lullaby against the leaded glass in the window. It had stopped by the morning, but the sky was grey, the air damp and misty. The fire had died down to just a few glowing embers, but as Cathryn lay in her bed, snuggling deep into the covers in pursuit of warmth, the door was quietly opened by a servant, coming to stoke up the flames. She returned a few minutes later with a cup of hot mulled wine and an offer to help Cathryn get ready for the day, an offer that Cathryn quickly accepted. She had not forgotten about her early morning ride with Margaret, and despite the inclement weather, was eager for the pursuit.

Warmly dressed, she descended the stairs a half hour later. Margaret was already awaiting her presence in the hall, and she greeted Cathryn with a warm smile.

"The horses are saddled and waiting, but we can remain indoors until the mist burns off if you prefer."

"No," responded Cathryn. "A little mist does not scare me, and it is bound to lift as we ride."

"Excellent," responded Margaret. "Then let us be off," she said, "the stables are not far." She led the way out the hall and into the courtyard. As they reached the stables, Cathryn could see the wilderness stretching into the distance ahead of them, while to the east lay the woods.

"We will follow the bridle path through the wilderness," said Margaret as she mounted her horse, "and then swing back through the woods. There is a pretty little pond where we can stop for a while."

Cathryn knew that many country estates allowed a few acres of their land to remain wild, although the name 'wilderness' was often misleading, since it was carefully cultivated. As they rode, she saw bright yellow daffodils dancing in the early morning breeze, while purple lupines and small white daisies added to the colorful display. The mist was starting to lift, revealing the sun hiding behind the curtains like a shy debutante. Birds sung out their chorus in the grass and bushes, and as they rode, Margaret pointed out robins, wrens, sparrows and woodpeckers flittering between the trees. A speck in the sky caught Cathryn's eye, and she looked up to see three shadows circling high in the air above them.

"Are those hawks?" she asked Margaret, directing her attention to the distant specks. Looking up, Margaret stared at the sky for a long time.

"They are too far away to see," she finally replied. "They may be hawks, or perhaps eagles. Too large for falcons, I think. You may see some other animals as we ride, though. Some deer, perhaps, or maybe a fox."

"What about wolves?" Cathryn asked.

"No, there aren't any wolves in these areas." Margaret pointed into the distance. "Can you see the swans? They will be landing in our little pond, which is not too far ahead." Following Margaret, Cathryn kicked her horse into a trot, and they quickly covered the distance to the pond, reaching it as the swans made their somewhat ungainly landing in the water, honking loudly as they did so.

The disturbance caused waves to lap against the edges of

the pond, causing water lilies to bob on the surface. A loud plop signaled the presence of a frog exiting into the water, while other water birds loudly proclaimed their annoyance at the intrusion. In just a few minutes, peace and calm had been restored, and Cathryn slid off her mount to examine the flowers and weeds growing at the water's edge. Small birds flew amongst the reeds, while dragonflies hovered over the water's surface, waiting for a tasty morsel. Butterflies flittered about, and with the peace restored, frogs climbed back onto the lily pads.

"It is so beautiful," said Cathryn quietly, afraid to disturb the peace once more. She watched as a mother duck took to the water from amongst the reeds, a brood of fluffy ducklings following in her wake. Their presence created barely a ripple as they moved smoothly through the water, diving their heads below the water's surface in search of food before bobbing back up once more. As she watched, Margaret moved around the pond, carefully collecting plants and flowers.

"Ah-ha," Margaret said with satisfaction as she broke off the stems of a plant with small white flowers. "Marsh mallow, useful in the treatment of many ailments." She moved to another tall-stemmed plant. "And this is yarrow, which prevents poisoning of the blood." Margaret's arms were soon filled with an abundance of plants, which she carefully placed in a saddle bag. Cathryn had found a log to rest on while Margaret scavenged, and she lifted her face to the warmth of the sun.

The air had grown hot by the time the two women turned their horses towards the woods, and the cool shadows were a welcome relief. Bluebells littered the ground along the path, while birds darted between the trees and squirrels scurried along the branches, chattering impatiently. In the distance Cathryn could hear the burbling of a stream, the sound a soothing background noise. They rode along in silence, the clip-clop of the horses' hooves against the well-trodden path the only sound foreign to the calm of the woods. As they rode, Cathryn found herself considering the woman riding before her. With her smooth skin, lustrous hair and straight back, she looked more like Favian's sister than his mother. And she and Owain seemed so happy together. How wonderful it must be to have parents such as these, Cathryn thought to herself. She could see where Favian had got his ideas of love and marriage. Perhaps, she thought, it is possible to truly love someone after all.

CHAPTER FIFTEEN

"Cathryn, my dear," said Margaret later that day, "I'm afraid I need to leave you to your own devices for a short while. One of our tenants has taken ill with fever, and I promised I would tend to her this afternoon."

"I'm happy to accompany you," offered Cathryn, but Margaret was adamant in her refusal.

"It may be a contagion, and I would not want to send you home ill."

"But you could contract the disease too," Cathryn protested.

"I have a very hardy constitution, my dear," she replied. "I always tend the tenants in their illnesses, and have never been ill a day in my life. I will be fine, but I do not want to risk your health."

Not wishing to argue further, Cathryn nodded her head in acquiescence. "Very well. Perhaps I will take a walk through the woods."

"Do you have a pair of walking boots? It may be a bit muddy." Margaret glanced at Cathryn as she nodded. "And you may see the gardener burning some rubbish."

Cathryn slipped into the courtyard a short while later, heading towards the woods in the distance. She had just reached the shade of the trees when she heard footsteps behind her. Turning around, she saw Favian following her along the path.

"Favian," she greeted. "Should I be concerned that you are following me into the woods?"

"Not at all," he responded. "I remain bound by my promise to act like a perfect gentleman." Cathryn lifted her eyebrows dubiously, and he let out a laugh. "Oh, you of little faith," he teased. "Actually, I wanted to return your hairpin."

"My hairpin?" she said in surprise. "When last I looked, it was nothing more than a lump of molten metal."

"Not at all," he said, pulling an object from a pocket. On his palm lay a hairpin, far more beautiful than anything she had ever seen. The pin itself had been made from bronze, but perched at the end now was a silver butterfly, measuring no more than half an inch across, its lacy wings open in flight. Lifting the pin from Favian's palm, Cathryn looked at it more closely. Each detail of the butterfly had been intricately wrought, no feature missing. It looked as though a tiny butterfly had been dipped in molten silver, capturing every element of the small creature.

"This is exquisite," breathed Cathryn. "Where did you get it?"

"I used the metal from your pin and fashioned a new one."

"You made this?" asked Cathryn. "It is so beautiful."

Favian shrugged. "Metalwork is a family talent."

"The pin is curved."

"That is to prevent it falling out so easily."

Cathryn turned it over in her hands, inspecting it more closely, before holding it out to Favian.

"I cannot accept this," she said.

"Why not?"

"Because … it would not be appropriate! I am betrothed to another man."

"Did I mention that this is actually a gift from my mother?" Favian said, his face unreadable. "She commissioned me to make it, and as she was going out, asked me to give it to you."

"Really?" said Cathryn, her tone filled with skepticism. She looked at the beautiful item once more, the appearance of fragility belying the strength of the delicately molded metal.

"Very well," she said with a grin, "I will be sure to thank her when she returns." Favian smirked back as she pulled her loose hair into a ponytail and twisted it into a bun.

"Let me," said Favian, taking her by the shoulders and turning her around. He gently pulled her hand away, allowing her hair to fall over her shoulders once more. Gathering it into his hands he pulled it together, twisting it as Cathryn had done before winding it in place. Taking the pin, he carefully pushed it through the thick coil of hair, securing it in place.

"You've had practice," she said, with a slight shiver as his warm breath caressed her skin.

"Perhaps," said Favian, gently running his fingers down her neck. The breath caught in her throat as instinctively she dropped her head slightly forward. She heard Favian's slight intake as he lightly traced his fingers across her skin, before dropping his hands and stepping away. Drawing in a wavering breath, she turned around to look at him. He was watching her, his expression intent, but as his gaze met hers, his mouth pulled up in a rueful smile. He watched her for another moment before turning his back to her and gazing out across the fields towards the house. Something in the distance drew his attention, and in a moment his body was alert and tense.

"Wait here," he said, his voice low, before striding away

from her. Confused, Cathryn looked past him in the direction he had been staring, pulling back into the shadows when she saw Aaron appear from around the house. He was marching towards Favian with long, purposeful strides, arms swinging and fists clenched. His brow was furrowed in anger, and his eyes were narrowed as he watched Favian draw closer. Stopping a few feet away from his cousin, Favian dropped his head. Raising his right arm, he placed a fist over his heart. To Cathryn, watching from beneath the trees, the gesture seemed deferential, but all sign of subservience disappeared when Favian lifted his head and crossed his arms over his chest, glaring down at his cousin. Although Aaron was a tall man, Favian topped his height by more than an inch. The two men glowered at each other for a moment, but it was Favian who spoke first. Cathryn was too far away to make out the words, but she could see both men stepping forward until they were nose to nose, each one tightly controlled as they swapped angry words. At one point Aaron gestured towards the trees, and Cathryn wondered whether she was the reason for this argument, although why Aaron had taken such a dislike to her, she couldn't fathom. A slight breeze wafted over her, bringing with it the occasional word, but not enough for her to follow the conversation. As she watched, Favian turned his back to his cousin and started walking away. Aaron said something to Favian's retreating back, but he ignored it. He spoke again as the breeze picked up, and this time Aaron's words reached her as clear as a bell.

"Does she know?" he said. Favian stopped, and lifting his head, looked across to where Cathryn stood, his eyes meeting hers over the distance. "You haven't told her, have you?"

Turning on his heel, Favian strode once more to where his cousin stood, and grabbing him by the arm, dragged him away in the opposite direction. Aaron pulled his arm from Favian's grasp, but kept pace with him as he marched towards a large clump of bushes and disappeared from sight. Cathryn stared at the bushes in confusion, wondering whether she should leave, when a burst of flame suddenly leapt up from behind the bushes, sending sparks flying into the air. She remembered Margaret saying that the gardener would be burning rubbish that afternoon, but was surprised that Favian would continue his argument in front of the man. The sparks were still drifting down when Favian came out from behind the bushes, striding towards her. He was alone, his head lowered as he frowned at the ground. His arms were crossed and his hand tapped out a steady beat against his upper arm as he walked. The muscles in his neck strained again his skin, and even from a distance Cathryn could see the tension in his jaw. As he approached, Favian dropped his hands to his sides and he looked up at her, the tension slowly draining from his body as he continued to draw near.

"My apologies for leaving you like that," he said. "Aaron won't be back, so do you mind if I join you on a walk? I thought perhaps I could show you a favorite place of mine."

Cathryn looked at him in consideration.

"Why does Aaron bear such an intense dislike towards me?" she asked.

"He's worried about my affection for you."

"Oh. Why?"

"He thinks love makes you weak and vulnerable."

"What was Aaron referring to when he asked if I knew?" she asked. Favian pulled his head back in surprise.

"I was not trying to eavesdrop," she defended herself, "but I could not help overhearing. He was referring to me, was he not?"

"Yes," said Favian reluctantly.

"And?" she prompted when he did not say anything more.

Favian contemplated her for a moment before slowly

77

responding.

"I do not believe I need to tell you," he said. "You have made it clear that we have no future together, which eliminates any need on my part to take you into my confidence. But perhaps," he continued, "you feel that the situation has changed?"

Cathryn looked down, uncomfortable, knowing that he was right. She should never have demanded this knowledge from him.

"No," she said. "Nothing has changed."

"Very well," he said. "Then let us consider the matter closed. I would still like to show you my favorite spot — are you up for the challenge?"

Cathryn glanced up, meeting the provocation in his amused gaze.

"Lead on," she replied.

CHAPTER SIXTEEN

It was cool under the trees, but Favian kept up a swift pace, and Cathryn found she was glad for the coolness. The mist from the morning had completely burned off, and the afternoon sun was hot.

"Am I going too fast for you?" Favian asked at one point, but she pointed to her boots and assured him she was managing fine. As they walked, Cathryn could hear the sound of a river getting closer as the temperature of the air dropped slightly. Favian had left the path, and was now winding his way through the trees towards the sound. The ground was slick with damp leaves, and Cathryn found herself grabbing for branches to steady herself as she walked.

"Nearly there," Favian called over his shoulder, and a moment later, after they rounded a small hillock, the river was in front of them. There was a bend in the river at the point where Favian had led them, the water rippling over large shallow rocks.

"Do you think you can manage a little scrambling?" Favian asked. He pointed a little further up the river to where a large flat rock jutted out from a rocky promontory and overhung the water rushing below. It was about ten feet above the ground, and Cathryn could make out a path cutting up from behind.

"I believe I can manage it," Cathryn replied, following Favian as he headed towards the back of the rocky outcrop. He climbed with ease, his long legs giving him an advantage, but for Cathryn, encumbered by long skirts and much shorter legs, the going was not quite as easy. With each new height, Favian stopped to pull her up and in this way, she managed to gain the rock he had pointed out.

Cathryn sank down next to Favian on the warm rock, and surveyed the surroundings. From this height she could see the river wending its way through the woods until it finally got lost in the thick of trees. Beyond the trees she could make out distant mountains, the peaks still white with snow.

"It is beautiful," Cathryn said. "Do you come here often?"

"As a boy, I used to spend all my time here. It was where I used to sit and contemplate the mysteries of life, and it had the added advantage that my sister never ventured this far into the woods!"

"I cannot imagine having that particular problem," Cathryn said with a laugh. "What is your sister like?"

"Ayleth and I share the same coloring, but that is where the similarity ends. We do not have much in common."

"I believe your mother said she's older than you?"

"That's correct," said Favian. "By eight years. Aaron and I used to play tricks on her, and she would rage for days. Not," he quickly added with a grin when he saw Cathryn raise her eyebrows, "that I condone that kind of thing, but boys will be boys."

"So Aaron also lived here?"

"No, he lived with his parents in a most marvelous castle." A slight frown crossed Favian's features, but was quickly smoothed away again. "But he frequently stayed here. He was also an only child," Favian smiled down at her, "and we were closer than brothers. When he was here, we were inseparable. This was one of our favorite places to play. We would swim and fish in the river, and sleep under the stars, and plan our futures."

"Are you still close?" asked Cathryn, remembering the anger between them earlier. Favian sighed, looking away at the mountains before responding.

"Aaron will always be my brother, but he has changed."

"What changed him?"

"Many years ago he saw his parents being slain by people in a nearby village. In one instant he lost all faith in humanity. He drew himself away, dwelling on thoughts of anger and revenge."

"Is that when he came to live with you?"

"No. He spent many years living alone, like a hermit. I found him a few years ago living in the mountains and forced him to come home. He does have his own estates, including Storbrook Castle, but he does not enjoy being trapped within their walls. Even when he comes here, he seldom stays in the chambers we keep for him."

"I'm sorry," said Cathryn, laying her hand on Favian's arm. Looking down at her hand, he reached his own over, intertwining his fingers with hers, before meeting her gaze.

"Like all of us, Aaron needs to find someone to love. But I am confident that he will."

Cathryn smiled at his optimism before gently pulling her hand away from his. The rock where they sat was high above the flowing river, swollen with the spring melt, and carefully leaning forward she watched as the water churned far below her dangling feet. A cloud passed over the sun, casting them into shadows, and she looked up with a shiver. High overhead a bird was circling, and she watched it for a moment.

"What kind of bird do you think that is?" she asked. Favian looked in the direction she pointed out, his eyes narrowing as he watched the bird in silence for a few minutes.

"That's not a bird," he finally said.

"It certainly is not a horse," she retorted. Favian glanced at her with a grin and then looked at the circling figure once more.

"It's a dragon," he said. It was still circling above them, dropping lower and lower with each turn, but it was too far for Cathryn to make it out clearly.

"Really?" said Cathryn, her tone dripping with skepticism. At her response, Favian looked down at her again, watching her until she returned his gaze. His expression was serious as he replied.

"Yes," he said. "Really. That is a dragon."

"Dragons aren't real."

Favian leaned in towards her until his face was only a few inches from hers.

"Yes, they are," he said, his tone gentle. He glanced back up at the circling figure, his jaw clenching as it dropped lower. As she watched, the creature looked down at them, and she gasped as she saw that Favian had been telling the truth. The creature circling above them was certainly no bird. As if to confirm this realization, the dragon opened its mouth and spewed flames into the air around it. Cathryn cringed back.

"That's a dragon," she whispered, her eyes wide as she stared at the creature above them. Her heart was pounding as she pushed herself to her feet with suddenly clammy hands, and a wave of nausea rolled over her. "We must get away before it eats us!" She looked around wildly, trying to locate the route they had taken to get to the top of the rock, but before she moved, Favian was on his feet. He grabbed her by the shoulders, forcing her to look at him.

"Cathryn, we are not in any danger." She was trembling beneath his hands as she looked at him with incomprehension.

"We've got to get away," she repeated, pulling herself free from his grasp. Once more he grabbed her by the shoulders, pulling her around to face him. She struggled against his hold, and he shook her gently.

"Cathryn," he said. He tightened his grip as she continued to struggle. "Cathryn," he repeated, his tone sharp, adding gently when she finally looked up at him, "we are not in any danger, I give you my word." She stared at him as the words slowly penetrated through her fear.

"How can you say that?" she demanded. "Look at that creature." She glanced back up to look at the dragon, still circling in the air above them. The light glanced off its scales, making it glow gold. "They breathe fire. And have horrible claws and tails. And they eat people."

"A short while ago you didn't even believe dragons existed, and now you are sure he wants to kill and eat you!" Favian looked at her incredulously. "Cathryn, dragons have lived around these lands for centuries, and never once has someone living here been in danger from them. You are perfectly safe. I will not allow any harm to come to you."

"Are you telling me that dragons don't eat people?" she demanded. Favian glanced away, his face troubled.

"I cannot make that assertion," he admitted. "Dragons sometimes do eat people, but I assure you, you are in no danger from this dragon. I will not allow you to come to any harm."

"What can you do against a dragon? Do you breathe fire? Do you have thick, scaly skin? Are you carrying a sword or spear with which to maim it? No! If that dragon chose to attack us, you would be just as vulnerable as me!" As though to give credence to her words, the dragon above gave out a mighty roar before spewing out a long, steady stream of flame. Sparks fell to the ground around them as they both looked up. Cathryn's face reflected her fear, but Favian glared at the creature in anger for a long moment, his eyes locking with the beast's.

"You have made your point," he said to the creature, "now leave us be!" More flames spewed from the mouth of the monster as a sound suspiciously like laughter floated down. Cathryn had broken free from Favian's grasp, and was scrabbling on the rocky path when Favian looked back down. Suppressing a sigh, he sprung down from the rock, landing gracefully on his feet ten feet below.

"Give me your hand," he said, stepping up on the first rock and reaching up. Cathryn looked down at him in surprise.

"How —?"

"I jumped. Now give me your hand." Cathryn tentatively lifted her hand from the rock she was leaning against and bent down to place it in Favian's, gasping when he pulled her with a jerk and caught her flying into his arms. He set her down on her feet, holding her shoulders until she regained her equilibrium.

"That was not necessary," she said sharply.

"I thought I would hasten your descent," he said, a slight smile playing on his lips. "You seemed anxious to get away from this place." Cathryn ground her teeth in annoyance, before marching towards the trees.

"This way," said Favian, catching up and placing his hand on her elbow. He glanced up at the sky once more before entering the shade of the leafy canopy, and moved ahead of Cathryn, leading the way through the mass of trees with long, intent strides. He walked in silence, glancing upwards occasionally, a frown furrowing his brow. They had reached the far edge of the woods before Favian slowed his pace, and he glanced over his shoulder at her before moving out into the open.

"Wait," she said. Favian paused to look back at her again. "Why are you so irate?"

"I must beg your forgiveness, Cathryn. I realize I am behaving with incredible rudeness, which you do not deserve."

"Of course," said Cathryn, "but are you angry at the dragon? You assured me that it was not a danger, and how can you be angry at a mindless beast?"

Favian laughed, a dry rasp that lacked all humor, but did not answer as Cathryn watched him thoughtfully.

"You don't consider it a mindless beast, do you?" she said slowly. "You believe it is capable of thought and intent — that the stories of the dragon's cunning and wile are true, then."

Favian glanced down at her, then looked away.

"No," he said, "you are right. The creature is just a mindless beast." He looked back at her. "We need to cross the wilderness to reach the house, but please do not be afraid. There is no danger from the dragon."

"Of course," said Cathryn, stepping out ahead of him. She glanced nervously up at the sky, but all she saw were a few white scuds of cloud. There was a pathway a little to the right, and she headed towards it, turning her direction towards the house in the distance, its' yellow stone gleaming in the sunlight. She heard Favian fall into step behind her as she walked. A bend in the path took them behind a cluster of trees, and as she rounded it, she was greeted by the sight of a fire up ahead, the gardener tossing piles of weeds onto the flames. She headed over to the blaze.

"Good afternoon," she said to the man.

"Mistress," the man greeted. He looked over her shoulder as Favian came up behind her. "Master," he said with a nod.

"You must have a lot to burn today," she said with a smile.

"Mistress?"

"I saw another fire closer to the house earlier."

"Wasn't me, Mistress. Wouldn't want'ta build a fire too close to the house," he said. "The wind could blow sparks onto the roof, you see."

"Oh." Cathryn turned to Favian. "I know I saw another

fire. It was behind the bushes where you were talking with Aaron. You must have seen it."

"Perhaps it was a dragon," the gardener said over his shoulder, turning back to the pile of dead rubbish.

"A dragon?" Cathryn turned a questioning look at Favian, who was staring at the gardener in stony silence. "Could it have been the dragon?"

"Did you see a dragon near the house?" he asked her, his eyes still eyeing the gardener narrowly.

"Well, no," she admitted.

"Then there is your answer. Come, let's go." He gestured with his hand for her to lead the way, following close behind when she did so. They walked in silence, and when they reached the house, Favian stopped.

"There is something I need to attend to, so I will ask you to excuse me. I believe my mother will have returned by now, and will be glad of your company." He gave her a brief smile before turning on his heel and striding away in the direction they had just come. Cathryn watched his retreating figure, sighing in frustration. The day seemed to be presenting a lot of questions, but absolutely no answers.

CHAPTER SEVENTEEN

Margaret was in the parlor, working on her needlepoint when Cathryn returned to the house. Taking a seat across from her, Cathryn took a moment to enquire after the patient.

"I think she will make a full recovery," Margaret said. "I gave her a tonic that will help relieve the pain and reduce the fever."

Cathryn nodded before continuing.

"Thank you for the lovely hairpin," she said.

"Hairpin?" said Margaret.

"Yes, look," said Cathryn, turning her head to show her the lovely piece. She turned back with a smile. "Favian said that you instructed him to give it to me."

"Ah, yes, of course! How forgetful I am becoming. You are most welcome, my dear." She met Cathryn's grin with a bland expression. "How was your afternoon?" she enquired.

"Interesting," said Cathryn. "Favian joined me as I was walking in the woods." She paused a moment. "We saw a dragon," she added.

"Ouch, look at that!" exclaimed Margaret, pulling a

bleeding finger away from her work. "How careless of me." Laying the canvas aside, she pulled a handkerchief from her pocket and dabbed the tiny wound. "A dragon, did you say?"

"Yes," said Cathryn. "I didn't even believe dragons existed before today. It seemed to make Favian very angry, however."

"He was probably concerned about the flocks," said Margaret, examining her finger closely.

"Maybe," said Cathryn, her tone doubtful. She watched Margaret as she continued to dab at her finger, her attention focused on the tiny puncture, before finally putting the handkerchief aside and picking up her needlepoint once more.

"Do you fear the dragon?" Cathryn asked.

"Fear it? No. The dragons around here would never intentionally hurt someone at Drake Manor."

"Dragons? How many are there?"

"I meant dragon, of course. Just one."

"So would the dragon hurt someone beyond Drake Manor?"

Margaret laid her needlepoint aside with a sigh, and looked at Cathryn.

"There is no need to fear the dragon, Cathryn. It will not hurt you."

"But how do you know that? It is a wild beast."

"You need to trust me when I say there is nothing to fear. I can say no more." Cathryn stared at Margaret as she picked up her needlepoint once more. She felt more confused than ever, and after another few minutes she excused herself and headed to her room.

Cathryn did not see Favian again that evening, and after a quiet meal, she retired to her room, pleading a headache. It had been a confusing, exhausting day, bringing with it a host of questions that remained unresolved, and she felt quite overwrought. She longed for the peace of a restful slumber, but sleep eluded her, and as the hours passed, she tossed and turned in her bed. She was still awake when Margaret and Owain climbed the stairs, their voices muted. They passed her room and moments later she heard the soft clicking of the door to their chambers.

Still later she heard other footsteps mount the stairs. They stopped outside her door, and she held her breath, listening. She thought she heard a hand laid gently on the door, but couldn't be sure, and a few moments later the person moved away, their footsteps fading down the passage.

She listened as the house creaked and groaned, settling itself for the night, before finally growing quiet as the servants found their pallets in the hall below and settled down to sleep. She heard an owl hooting in a tree near her window, and she shivered, remembering the night she had walked with her father from the Bradshaws'. Was there a dragon in the alley that night? she wondered. The questions kept coming as the events of the day slipped through her exhausted mind, mulling around like the ingredients in a witches' brew, conjuring uncanny thoughts but bringing no answers.

The sky was already starting to lighten when she finally fell into a restless sleep, the thoughts pursuing her into her dreams. She was trapped, surrounded by flames while overhead a dragon was roaring, flying closer and closer in tight circles, its claws extended as it neared her. There was no escape from the flames, and she looked around in terror. Beyond the flames stood Aaron and Favian, one on either side. "Favian," she cried out, "help me." He stood with his arms crossed over his chest, and looked at her with an odd mixture of pity and disdain. "Help me," she cried again, and watched in horror as he opened his mouth and breathed out a stream of flames that added to her prison. She turned in terror and saw Aaron watching her, a cruel smile on his face. He stood with his arms at his sides, and throwing his head back, breathed out his own stream of flame. Above them the dragon looked down and met Aaron's flames with his own, creating a massive wall that reached high into the sky. She saw Favian walk around to Aaron, and heard the words *my brother*, his fiery laugh joining with Aaron's as they both stared at her. She shrank back, away from the heat, and collapsed onto the cold ground, shivering. She rolled herself tightly into a small ball and covered her head with her hands, crying for mercy, but instead all she heard was the sound of cruel laughter and the stamping of feet, pounding the ground. The stamping grew louder, a hammering that finally penetrated through the dreadful images that had taken hold of her mind, and she realized that she was lying on the cold stone floor of her bedroom while a fist pounded on the door.

"Cathryn," she heard Margaret call out. "Cathryn, are you all right?"

It was just a dream, she thought to herself. She pushed herself up to her knees before slowly rising to her feet. Her cheeks were streaked with tears and she scrubbed them with her hands. She heard Margaret calling again.

"Coming," she said, her voice a broken whisper. "Coming," she said again. She pulled her wrap over her shoulders and opened the door. At the sight of her, Margaret grabbed her hands in relief.

"Are you all right, my dear? We heard you cry out, and I've been pounding on the door for nigh on five minutes."

"Yes," said Cathryn wearily, "just a bad dream." She saw Margaret look down the passage and nod her head, and she leaned forward to see who was there, drawing back in embarrassment when she saw Favian and Owain standing in the passage, their faces etched with concern. Turning her around, Margaret led Cathryn to the bed.

"Do you want to talk about it?" Margaret asked gently.

"Not really," said Cathryn. "I was dreaming about dragons … and fire."

"Ah," said the older woman. "I heard you call for Favian."

"He did not help," replied Cathryn, dully. Margaret watched her for a moment.

"You are exhausted. Lie back down, and I will send for some mulled wine with some lemon balm. It will soothe your mind and perhaps allow you a few hours of rest."

Cathryn did as she was bid, and a few minutes later a servant appeared with a wooden cup in her hand. Cathryn drank down the contents as Margaret watched, then lay back on the pillows.

"Try and get some rest, my dear."

Cathryn watched as Margaret exited the room, and listened to her footsteps as they echoed down the hall. Owain and Favian must still be waiting, she realized, because she heard the murmurings of voices from that direction. The sounds were soothing and she closed her eyes, finally surrendering to a dreamless sleep, just as the sun started to appear on the horizon.

CHAPTER EIGHTEEN

The sun was high in the sky when Cathryn finally awoke. The few hours of sleep had restored some of her calm, and she allowed herself a few moments of blissful idleness before sitting up in her bed. Someone had been in while she slept and stoked up the fire, and she felt the warmth blazing through the room.

All was quiet when she made her way downstairs a short while later. A quick glance in the parlor and dining rooms showed that no-one was present, and her footsteps echoed through the empty hall as she crossed the room looking for signs of life. As she retraced her footsteps and headed back into the passage, the sound of low voices reached her, and she paused to look out into the courtyard. In the far corner stood Favian and Owain, conversing with Aaron. As she watched she saw Favian lift his head, and then turn quickly in her direction. She pulled back into the shadows, but he was already heading towards her, covering the distance in quick strides and swinging his legs over the low wall that separated them.

"How are you this morning?" he asked softly.

Cathryn looked down, the heat rising in her cheeks,

mortified that she had been the cause of so much commotion, but placing a finger beneath her chin, he forced her head up and looked into her eyes.

"Please don't feel embarrassed," he said softly. "I feel partly responsible for your unpleasant night." He held up a hand when she started to protest. "I allowed my anger to get the better of me yesterday, adding to your distress after seeing the dragon."

"It was not your fault," Cathryn tried to assure him. "It was the result of an overactive mind. And maybe the realization that dragons are real," she added with a nervous laugh.

Favian grimaced, before staring across the courtyard to where Owain and Aaron were still talking. He watched them for a moment before returning his attention to Cathryn.

"My mother went to visit her patient, but she should return soon. She left instructions for your dinner to be kept aside. Should I send for it?"

Cathryn allowed Favian to escort her to the dining room, and he sent for her food, sitting himself down at the table to keep her company while she ate.

"Cathryn," he said, "I find that I have a need to go into town, so I will accompany you when you return later today."

"Oh?" she said with an amused glance up at him. "Does this need have something to do with a dragon?" He gazed at her for a moment, his own expression serious, before responding.

"I told you that you have nothing to fear from the dragon we saw, and that remains the truth, but I would feel better knowing that you are not traveling unattended."

"You could send a servant," she suggested.

"A servant would be as fearful as you," he said, "should the dragon make an appearance."

"But you are not scared of the dragon?" she asked.

"No."

"And could you battle with it if the need arose?"

"Yes."

"Hmm. Very well," she said, "I will accept your escort." At this Favian grinned, knowing as well as she did that her acquiescence was merely for form's sake. "Perhaps," she continued, "we could make good use of the time and start negotiating the sale of your fleeces."

"Indeed, Mistress, but be warned that I drive a hard bargain."

"I look forward to the challenge," she said, glancing up as Margaret entered the room.

"Dear Cathryn, how are you feeling this morning?" she asked, taking a seat beside her. Cathryn nodded, replying that she felt much better, as Favian pushed himself from the table and stood up.

"Ladies," he said, giving a shallow bow before exiting the room.

A few hours had passed by the time Cathryn was ready to take her leave of Drake Manor. She clasped Margaret's hands as she stood outside the door.

"Thank you for everything," she said with a smile. "I have enjoyed my stay very much. I can only apologize for causing so much fuss."

"Nonsense," replied Margaret, "there is nothing to apologize for. Your company has been very welcome, and I hope you will soon return for a longer stay."

"I would like that," Cathryn said She glanced at Owain, who was watching her with an indulgent smile. "Master Drake, thank you for your kind hospitality."

"You have brought excitement to our dull existence," he said with a grin as Margaret tutted and smacked his hand lightly. Placing his hands on Cathryn's shoulders he pulled her against his chest. She stood tense for a moment, and then relaxed into his fatherly embrace, smiling at him when he pulled away.

"We all look forward to your imminent return, Cathryn." His gaze met Favian's for a moment. "As Margaret has already said, your next stay must be longer."

Cathryn nodded. "Thank you," she said.

She turned to the carriage and stepped into its confines, Favian close on her heels. He pulled the door closed behind him and leaned back in the seat, adjusting himself as the carriage lurched into movement.

"So where do we begin?" he said.

"With your two thousand Lincolns," she replied. She smiled sweetly as she started plying him with questions about his flock. On what kind of land did the sheep graze? When were the sheep sheared? How consistent was the color of the flock?

"I will need to see a sample of the wool before I can make you an offer," she finally said.

"Of course," he replied, "I will call on you with samples in the coming days."

"I will be heading out on the road soon," she reminded him.

"I hadn't forgotten," he said. He leaned back in the seat and regarded her for a moment. "You clearly are very knowledgeable about wool production, and the worth of fleeces."

"Of course. I grew up in the business. From the time I was a child, I have been taught everything I needed to know."

"Everything you need to know about being a wool merchant, perhaps," he said.

"What do you mean?" she asked. He leaned forward in his seat, bringing his face closer to hers.

"Cathryn, you have been schooled so well with regard to the business, that it did not even occur to you to question whether you should be married to further your father's business prospects."

"Marriages based on business alliances are made every

day," she protested.

"Yes, but Cathryn, you accepted your fate with complete equanimity, without any consideration for your own personal happiness. You are not a princess, involved in high-stakes politics, or the daughter of the titled gentry, seeking to expand their influence. The advantages gained by your marriage to Beaumont can be obtained through other means, without you sacrificing your happiness." Cathryn glared at him as he spoke.

"I thought we had agreed to a truce."

"The truce ended when we left Drake Manor," he said, "and now I will have my say." Reaching over, he took her hands within his own, holding them tight when she would have pulled away. He stared down at them for a moment before lifting his gaze to hers. "From the moment I first met you, that day in the rain, I knew that you were the one my heart had been searching for. It was not that you are a beautiful woman — I have met many beauties and yet never felt this way. And it was not because you fell into my arms, as much as I enjoyed that. Rather, it was a rightness that settled into my bones." Cathryn drew in a breath, feeling her heart quicken at his words. "But when I realized that you were not only betrothed, but to a man such as Geoffrey Beaumont, I thought I must be mistaken. I tried to put you from my mind, but the memory of you would not give me peace. And so I watched you, those first few days." He smiled in amusement when her eyebrows flew up in surprise. "And in observing," he continued, "I quickly came to the conclusion that your attachment to Beaumont was not one of affection. And I was sure that as much as you were in my mind, I was in yours. You insist you feel nothing for me, but your denials are futile — we both know them to be falsehoods. We are meant to be together, Cathryn. Allow yourself to admit the truth. Put aside this betrothal and marry me instead."

Cathryn pulled in a sharp breath, and Favian tightened

his grip around her hands. "Don't say anything now. Just give me your word that you will consider it."

"But we have a contract," she whispered.

"Contracts can always be undone," he said. "I will make full reparation to your father and to Beaumont for any financial burden this may impose on them personally or on their respective businesses."

"But —" she started, but he placed his fingers over her mouth.

"Shhh," he said, "say nothing more now. Just give me your word you will think on what I have said."

Her eyes were wide as she stared at him before finally nodding in response.

"I love you," he said, lowering his hand from her mouth. Pulling her hand to his lips, he gently kissed her fingers before letting go. He leaned back in his seat as Cathryn looked down at her hands, uncomfortable. She cursed herself for being lulled into complacency in his company, even as she recognized the truth of what he was saying. She could no longer deny what she felt for him, and yet … was it enough? She glanced up to see him watching her intently, and she looked away once more, drawing the curtain from the window and staring, unseeing, at the countryside rushing by. She could feel the weight of his stare, and twitched nervously. Eventually it became too much to bear, and she turned back to look at him with a furious glare.

"It was very ungentlemanly of you to make your declarations while I was trapped in a carriage," she said angrily. Favian laughed.

"As I have told you before, my love, I am no gentleman."

"Then what are you?" she demanded. "A rogue? A cad? A thief?"

"I am many things," he said, "but none of those are important. All that matters is that I love you, and you love me."

"Urgh," she said, "you are incorrigible!"

"Take heart, my love," he said, "we are almost in town. You will be rid of me soon enough."

"Thank goodness for small mercies."

"Don't get too grateful," he said with a laugh, "you will be seeing plenty of me in the coming days. Don't forget that you promised to give thought to my proposal, and," he said, leaning forward and dropping his voice, "I will not accept 'no' as an answer." She shivered as she looked away.

"Incorrigible," she muttered.

CHAPTER NINETEEN

"How was your visit?" Father asked later that evening.

"It was most interesting."

"Interesting? How so?"

Cathryn watched her bangle gleam in the candlelight as she twisted it around her wrist. She looked up to meet her father's curious gaze. "Margaret has a lovely garden, and is very knowledgeable about herb lore."

"Oh. Well, yes, I suppose that could be interesting. And did you enjoy yourself?"

"Yes. Margaret Drake is a lovely woman, and I enjoyed extending our acquaintance."

"And Master Drake? What kind of man is he?"

Which one? Cathryn thought sardonically. "Master Drake seems to be a good man. And he owns two thousand Lincolns."

"Ah! You contracted to buy the fleeces, I'm sure." Cathryn met her father's amused gaze with a smile of her own.

"Of course." She pushed herself up from her seat. "Now if you will excuse me, I think I will retire early."

Once in her chambers, Cathryn sank down onto her

bed. Favian's proposal had been lingering at the edge of her thoughts, and in the solitude of her room it came rushing to the fore. She could no longer ignore his feelings for her, nor her own for him. She knew what her heart was saying. The only question, really, was whether she could trust her heart. Could she be sure that it was not leading her down a fickle path that would lead to misery and torment? Cathryn rose at the sound of the door opening, and watched as Hannah entered the room.

"How was your visit?" Hannah asked, picking up a brush and pointing at the stool. Cathryn sat down.

"I had a most enjoyable time with Madame Drake," Cathryn said.

"And what about Master Drake? Was he there too?"

"Master Drake?" Cathryn spun around to look at Hannah.

"It was Master Drake who came to call a few weeks ago, was it not?" Cathryn met Hannah's amused gaze, and turned around on the stool.

"Yes."

"Did you have opportunity for private conversation?"

Cathryn closed her eyes. "Yes." She paused. "He wants me to marry him."

"Marry? Does he know about your betrothal?"

"Yes."

"What did you say?"

"I promised to think upon it."

Hannah pulled the butterfly pin from Cathryn's braid, and brought it closer to examine it.

"This is beautiful. Where did you get it?"

"It was a gift from Margaret Drake." Cathryn met Hannah's gaze in the mirror. "It was crafted by Favian Drake."

"Ah!" They fell into silence for a few minutes as Hannah pulled the brush through Cathryn's hair, making it gleam in the candlelight. "Do you love him?"

Cathryn dropped her face into her hands. "Yes," she whispered.

"Then you already have your answer," Hannah said.

Cathryn thought about Hannah's words as she lay in bed some time later. Was it really so simple?

The moon was dropping in the night sky when a slight wind picked up, blowing open the shutters. Cathryn shivered in her sleep as the tenor of her dreams changed. Once again, Aaron stalked through her dreams while dragons roamed through the sky. She tossed and turned, mumbling in her sleep, seeking a refuge from the beast that pursued her. A gust of wind banged the shutter against the wall, and Cathryn woke with a start, searching the room wide-eyed for fire-breathing monsters, before falling back on her pillows. Another dream, she thought. It seemed she could not escape either Aaron or the dragon. The dream was already fading, but something teased at the edges of her mind. She closed her eyes and reached, trying to grasp the disappearing tendrils — there was something in the dream she needed to remember, but already it was gone.

Cathryn pulled the quilt up around her ears, trying to find sleep once more, but the wind was banging the shutter repeatedly against the wall. After a few minutes, she abandoned the effort to sleep and rose from her bed. The sky was already lightening as she leaned out the window to secure the offending covering. A few clouds scudded through the heavens, but they were quickly being pushed aside by the force of the wind. After a swift debate, Cathryn turned away from the window and dragged on her riding habit, tugging the stays at her side tight before pulling on her sturdy boots. She crept down the stairs and quietly let herself out the door and onto the street.

Once again Cathryn had to rouse a sleeping stable boy, but the promise of a shiny coin quickly brought him to his feet, and within a few minutes Cathryn was trotting down the street on Morana's back. She lifted her chin into the wind and shook her hair loose as she left the town gates behind her, letting the breeze catch the tendrils and toss them around her face. She slackened the reins as soon as she reached the meadow, and the horse whickered into the wind as it gathered speed. She could see the oak tree in the distance, a dark smudge against the grey sky. After a brief gallop, Cathryn pulled in her mare and slowed her to a trot. There was a rider in the distance, traveling in her direction, and he slowed as he drew near. The light was still too dim to see the features clearly, but Cathryn could make out a man riding the back of a very large stallion. His horse was fidgety and unsettled, uncomfortable with the weight on its back. The pair drew closer, and Cathryn drew in a breath when she recognized Favian coming towards her.

"What are you doing here?" she demanded.

"Good morning, my love!" he said with a grin. "I could ask the same of you."

"I often ride in the morning," she said with a toss of her head, "but I have never seen you out here before."

"I found myself unable to sleep," he explained, "and thought a ride would help clear my thoughts."

"Do I dare enquire why you couldn't sleep?" she asked cheekily.

"You can ask, but I will not give you an answer," he said. "Now your turn — why are you out so early?"

"I found myself unable to sleep," she replied, "and thought a ride would help clear my thoughts." Favian laughed.

"Touché," he said.

"Is that your horse?" she asked as it snorted and flicked its tail beneath him.

"No, I rented him from the stables," he said. He leaned down and patted the horse on the neck, but the action did nothing to quiet the animal. "He's not very calm, but I can guarantee that he's fast. Do you want to race to that oak at the end of the meadow?"

"Race?" she exclaimed in horror. "A lady does not race!"

Favian pulled back in surprise. "My apologies, Cathryn. I did not mean to suggest you were not —"

He kicked his horse into motion as Cathryn flew out ahead of him, her laughter trailing on the wind behind her. She reached the tree first, and reined Morana in sharply before sliding off her back.

"Yes?" she said with a sweet smile as Favian reined in beside her. "I did not catch what you were saying."

"You," he said as he jumped off the horse, "are a very sneaky woman." She took a step back as he stalked towards her, but the tree behind her gave her no leeway for escape. "I think," he continued, placing his hands on the tree trunk on either side of her head, "I will have to re-evaluate your character."

"Really?" she said, but the word came out in a breathy waver. He was so close, his eyes intent on her. Flecks of yellow burned deep within his eyes, and she watched, mesmerized, as he brought his face closer. Her lips opened, and then his mouth was on hers, sending a flame of heat rushing through her. Wrapping a hand around her neck, he pulled her closer, tangling his hand in her hair and keeping her captured. Her hands slipped around his back, lingering for a moment before sliding up towards his shoulders, caressing the taut muscle and sinew just beneath his skin. She could feel his warmth through the thin fabric of his tunic, and pressed herself even closer, curling her body into his. His lips moved away from hers, trailing over her neck, before he pulled away slightly, looking down into her eyes. .

"Does this mean you are ready to give me an answer," he asked softly. She dropped her head back to the tree trunk behind her, her heart pounding in her chest. His gaze held hers as he waited for an answer, and she smiled up at him, before twisting away in a quick movement, slipping under his arm with a laugh.

"Perhaps," she said, "but then again, perhaps not."

"Tell me," he said, turning around and leaning back against the tree, "did you dream about me last night?"

"That would be telling," she teased, "but I will tell you this: I dreamt about your cousin."

"Aaron?" His face grew concerned. "Did you have another nightmare?"

"No," she said slowly, "I don't think so. It was a strange dream, but not like before."

"Tell me," he said.

"I don't really remember it," she replied. The eastern sky was glowing with the colors of sunrise, and Cathryn turned to watch. "Aaron was in it, as was the dragon. I woke up in the middle of the dream, but as soon as I awoke, I felt as though I was missing something. That there was something I should know about the dragon, but it kept eluding me." She turned to look at Favian, who was watching her silently.

"What do you think it means?" she said.

"I think it means that you are still afraid of the dragon."

"No, it's something more, I know it. There is something I know about the dragon, but just cannot remember."

"Cathryn, what do you know about dragons? Just a few days past you didn't even believe they existed!"

"Well, I know what I've heard in the stories," she said.

"Stories," scoffed Favian. "There's very little truth in stories."

"I know that dragons are fierce monsters."

"Only some of them."

"I know they eat innocent maidens."

"Pure fabrication."

"I know they breathe fire," she continued.

"Well, yes, that's true," he admitted.

"And have tails with spikes that can mortally injure someone." Favian shrugged his concurrence.

"And ..." Cathryn cast her mind back to the night at the

Bradshaws', trying to recall what else the bard had said about dragons. "Dragons can ..." Her eyes widened as the story came rushing back.

"Yes?" Favian prompted.

"Dragons can take on the form of man," she whispered, taking a step back. She looked up at Favian, looking for confirmation, and saw the expression freeze on his face as he stared at her.

"Is that true?" she whispered, but Favian remained silent.

"Aaron," she gasped, "Aaron is ... Aaron is a dragon, isn't he?" Still Favian remained silent, his face set like stone.

"But how ...? He's your cousin!" She stared at Favian, the color draining from her face as she took another step backwards.

"Cathryn," he said, taking a step towards her, but she held up her hand, stumbling as she backed away from him.

"No," she whispered, "tell me it's not true. Tell me you're not ... not a dragon."

"Cathryn."

"Tell me!" Her voice rose as she repeated the words. "Tell me!"

"I can't," he whispered.

"No! No!"

"Please, listen to me," he said, moving towards her with his hands outstretched.

"Don't touch me," she screamed. "Stay away from me." Turning on her heel she ran towards Morana, throwing herself over the saddle and hitching her leg over with a gasp.

"Cathryn," he shouted, running after her. "Stop!"

Cathryn's booted heels kicked into the horse's flanks, spurring the animal into motion as Favian reached to catch the reins, missing them by less than an inch. Cathryn reached down and hugged Morana's neck as she sped past Favian, tears streaming down her face. She kicked the horse again, urging her to go even faster, shuddering when she heard a roar ripping through the air behind her. She did not dare look back, but kept her head down as she raced towards the town as it slowly wakened to a new day.

CHAPTER TWENTY

Cathryn sat at a small desk in her chambers, staring down at the paper in front of her which listed the items still needing to be completed before she started her tour. Father had finally agreed that the weather had settled enough for the roads to be passable, and with just two days to go before they left, there was still much to be done. She looked up as Hannah entered the room.

"Master Drake is here again. Should I send him away?"

"Yes." Hannah watched Cathryn for a moment before nodding and leaving the room. Cathryn stared at the door after it closed. Favian had come by every day since that fateful morning when she discovered what he really was. She thought back to the conversation she'd had with Hannah the first time he called, when she told Hannah that she would not see him.

"Why not?" Hannah had demanded.

"He is not the man he appears to be," Cathryn replied.

"Did he hurt you?"

"No."

"Then what is it? Is he running from the law?"

"No. Nothing like that. He's a good man. I just cannot

marry him."

"But ... I don't understand."

"Please, Hannah," Cathryn had said. "Just let it be."

The sound of a door closing brought her back to the present. She rose and walked over to the window, looking down on the street below. Favian appeared from beneath the overhang, and she pulled into the shadows as he paused. Turning slowly, he looked up at the window of her chambers, his eyes searching. They stopped when he reached the corner where she stood, although she was sure he could not see her in the shadows. "I love you," she saw him say. He stared for another moment, then dropped his gaze and slowly turned away. The tears gathered in her eyes and spilled unheeded down her cheeks as she watched him walk down the street.

Although Cathryn pushed all thought of him away while she was awake, she could not prevent him from pursuing her into her dreams. She dreamt of him every night. Sometimes the dreams were filled with warm embraces and words of love. He would hold her tight and whisper her name into her hair, before capturing her lips with his own, and she would wake in the morning with a wistful yearning.

But other times the dreams were filled with frustration.

"Why?" the dream Favian would demand. "Why can you not love me?"

"Because you are a dragon," she would whisper.

"What does it matter?" he would say, but she had no answer.

On the morning of their departure, Hannah coiled Cathryn's hair into a knot, securing it with the butterfly pin. Cathryn opened her mouth to protest, but slowly closed it again when she caught Hannah's gaze in the mirror. She pulled the silver bangle onto her wrist, and waited as Hannah tightened the stays on her habit. A few minutes later she descended the stairs, Hannah following a few steps behind. The trunks had already been stowed in one of the wagons, along with all the other provisions for the trip. She stepped out of the house, and with the help of Felix, mounted Morana while Hannah climbed onto the seat of the wagon, waiting in the lane. It was a sunny day, and Cathryn glanced up at the sky to see only a few fluffy puffs that bore no threat of rain. High overhead she saw a dark shape circling above them — bird or dragon, she could not say — and she quickly glanced away.

"Ready?" she asked Felix, who responded with a nod. Father was holding her reins, and he reached up to pat her hand before stepping back. She gave him a quick smile as she set her horse in motion, Felix falling into step beside her. They soon reached the town's gates, where the rest of the convoy were waiting to join them. Twelve wagons in total, ready to be filled with bundles of fleeces, each with a driver and an outrider who rode beside the wagon. Once each wagon was fully loaded with fleeces it would return with the goods to the warehouse in town.

They made good progress the first day, traveling along a well-worn road. The first destination was a monastery, half a day's ride away when the distance was traveled on a fast mount, but almost two days away when traversed by a large convoy. Once there, the monks would offer rooms to the travelers; but for the first night, they stopped at a small wayside inn where they were offered a bowl of greasy stew and a straw pallet. Cathryn, to her relief, was given a small room which she shared with Hannah, but the men were bedded in the large common room, the tables and benches pushed against the wall.

After an uncomfortable night, they were up early the following morning, hitching the wagons and saddling the horses. Another long day of riding saw them approaching the monastery at nightfall. A forerunner had been sent on ahead to warn the abbot of their imminent arrival, and as the convoy neared the sprawling buildings, Cathryn found that their arrival was expected. Business conversations would wait until the morrow, but for now the promise of a warm meal and comfortable bed cheered them for the evening.

Eight hundred fleeces were ready to be loaded onto a wagon the following morning, a task completed while Cathryn and the abbot conducted their business, and the convoy was ready to set off once more by noon. The next destination was a large market town, where small fleece lots could be purchased from tenant farmers.

The days and weeks that followed started to blur as Cathryn continued her tour. Some nights were spent at wayside inns of varying quality and service, while other nights were spent at fine estates or austere monasteries where Cathryn took delivery of fleeces, drew up contracts or renegotiated old ones. At one estate the owner was unable to produce the required number of fleeces, and when Cathryn suggested that they renegotiate the contract on terms less advantageous to him, he grew belligerent. Cathryn was sure it was only due to Felix's presence that she escaped without physical injury.

They had been on the road for fifteen days when the company was forced to put up camp on the roadside. The light was already starting to fade when the forerunner returned with the news that the next town was still twelve miles away, too far to reach before nightfall. A quick consultation with Felix resulted in the decision to stop alongside the road for the night, and he moved on ahead to scout out a suitable place to camp. He returned within a few minutes, indicating that there was a suitable site under some trees less than a mile ahead. They had just reached the spot when the sound of racing hooves was heard over the sounds of the creaking wagons and plodding horses. Turning in her saddle, Cathryn looked back to see a rider approaching them from behind. Next to her, Felix waved his hand, indicating that the convoy should stop to allow the rider to pass, but as he drew nearer he began to slow down. It was not until he was close that a gasp escaped Cathryn.

"Geoffrey," she said, "whatever are you doing here?" Eyes sparkling with humor, Geoffrey bowed in her direction, managing to look elegant despite being covered in dust and seated atop a horse.

"Cathryn," he said with a warm smile, "I came to keep you company."

"Whatever for?"

"Perhaps I wanted to spend some time with you," he said with a grin. Cathryn stared at him and her mouth hung open, until she clamped it shut with a snap.

"Has something happened?" she finally asked as Geoffrey urged his horse closer.

"Nothing that I'm aware of," he said. He glanced around, noting the stationary wagons. "Where are you headed?" he asked.

"Actually," said Cathryn, a slight smile tugging her lips, "we are about to set up camp." Geoffrey groaned as she continued. "Would you like to join us?"

"Definitely not," he said with a shudder. "I will proceed to the next town and await you there." He paused for a moment before continuing. "You could always come with me, and await the arrival of your convoy on the morrow."

"Certainly not," replied Cathryn smartly. "I would be risking more than my reputation if I were to go with you."

"Cathryn," said Geoffrey in an aggrieved tone, "whatever do you take me for? I never force a lady against her will. And we are to be married, so there really isn't any risk."

"I will see you on the morrow," she said in a firm tone. "I look forward to hearing what in heaven's name you are doing here."

CHAPTER TWENTY-ONE

Cathryn lay on her mat, absently twisting the bangle on her wrist as she watched the stars shining brightly in the dark sky. Hannah lay next to her, while Felix was a few feet away. The rest of the men lay on the other side of the fire, far away from the two women.

"Why do you think Master Beaumont followed you?" Hannah whispered, turning on her side to face Cathryn.

"I cannot imagine," Cathryn whispered back. "I can only think he must bring some news, but he did not seem pressed with a sense of urgency."

"Perhaps he wanted to see you."

Cathryn muffled a laugh.

"We both know better than that."

Cathryn was stiff and cold when she awoke the following morning. She pulled the quilt around her shoulders as she sought some extra warmth. There were clouds building on the horizon and she watched them, concerned that they would bring rain. A movement in the sky caught her attention, and she looked to see a shape circling above her. It had been there every day, circling so high it was nothing more than a dark smudge against blue, but this morning she could clearly see the large wings of the creature. Cathryn watched it for a moment, refusing to contemplate what kind of creature it was, before throwing off the quilt and pushing herself to her feet. A fire was already roaring within a ring of stones, and she went to stand before it, rubbing her cold hands together. A pot had been suspended on sticks above the flames, and a thick sludge of oats and water bubbled lazily above the heat. Seeing that Cathryn was up, Felix pushed a spoon through the heavy liquid, and plopped the contents into a wooden bowl which he handed to her. For a moment, the contents held their shape, before oozing outwards to cover the bottom of the bowl. Cathryn nodded her thanks, and finding a log, she sat down to eat in silence.

It was already early afternoon by the time the convoy rolled into the little town, Cathryn at its lead. The noise of the wagons drew people to their windows, and as they pulled up alongside a coaching house, she saw Geoffrey emerge.

"You look like you could make good use of a cloth and bowl of water," he said by way of greeting, eyeing her dusty clothes and disheveled hair with poorly disguised distaste.

"Good afternoon to you too," she replied, handing her reins to Felix and entering the inn, Hannah close on her heels.

"Clean yourself up," he said. "I will await your pleasure in the taproom."

"It may take a while." A flick of the hand was her only response. She turned to see the innkeeper watching her.

"A room for me and my maid, a stack of linens, fresh clean water, and a cup of wine," she ordered.

When Cathryn descended the stairs an hour later, Geoffrey was waiting in the taproom. He threw a handful of coins onto the bar and pushed himself away from the counter.

"Come along," he said, taking her by the arm and

pulling her out of the room. "Let's take a walk."

"Where are we going?" she asked.

"Away from here," he replied. "I need to discuss something with you."

"What is so important that you could not await my return?" she asked as they walked along the lane. A small stone church stood at the end of the road, and he led her into the gardens, weaving his way between weathered headstones and sculptured stone angels.

"You expressed a desire to hasten our marriage," he said, glancing her way as he spoke, "and after giving it some consideration, I have concluded that you are correct. There is no point in our waiting any longer to finalize the marriage contract." Cathryn stopped, staring at him in surprise.

"I don't understand," she said after a moment. "Why did you feel you needed to convey this change of heart before my return?" They had reached a line of bushes which marked the perimeter of the church yard. Ducking his head, Geoffrey pushed his way through a narrow opening, holding the branches back as Cathryn followed. Open fields lay before them, a footpath wending its way towards the distance.

"Why wait until you return to town?" he said. "We will be married right away and return to town as man and wife."

"What? Why would we do that?" She rubbed her fingers over her forehead. "A few weeks ago you seemed quite adamantly opposed to getting married in the near future, and now you cannot wait? What are you up to, Geoffrey?"

"Nothing at all," he replied, stepping up to her. "You need to learn to trust me, my dear. Maybe I am just eager to be married to you."

"Hmph," said Cathryn, turning her back to him. "I will believe that when the moon turns blue."

"Well then, I thought I could lend you support while you are on the road."

Cathryn turned to look at him suspiciously.

"Why?"

"Why not," said Geoffrey, suddenly exasperated. "This is what you wanted, isn't it? To finalize the marriage?"

"Yes," said Cathryn, "but not like this, as though we have something to hide."

"No-one will think that," said Geoffrey. "This is a long-standing business arrangement, and it is in our best interests to conclude the matter now." He took a step towards Cathryn, his eyes suddenly soft and beseeching. He took her hand in his own and gently brought it to his lips, kissing each finger in turn. Still holding it, he leaned in to whisper. "Please, my dear, I have followed you for days, wanting to have you by my side. Would you deny me now?" He wound his hand around her neck and pulled her closer, while his fingers trailed down her cheeks. "I'm very fond of you," he said, bringing his lips closer, "and I want to feel you in my arms." His lips descended onto hers, and for a moment Cathryn stood frozen, before she pushed him away.

"What are you doing?" she demanded.

"Cathryn," he said, "we are about to be married."

"We are not about to be married," she said, turning away. She felt his fingers slipping down her back and landing on her waist, where they lingered a moment before pulling her around to face him. His lips descended onto hers once more, soft at first, then becoming more demanding as he pulled her against him, holding her tight against his chest. She tried to pull herself free, but his hand slipped up her back to her head, preventing her retreat. She felt her hair fall around her shoulders as the pin tumbled out of its knot, and for a moment she panicked at the thought of it being broken, but as he forced her mouth open with his tongue, all thoughts except halting his attentions fled from her mind. A kick at his shins slackened his grasp, and she pulled away as a loud roar suddenly sounded above them. She looked up and screamed when she saw a dragon diving out of the sky straight towards them.

A quick glance up and Geoffrey was turning on his heel, but he could not outrun the dragon. The creature landed on the ground beside them, and with one quick flash of a talon, knocked Geoffrey to the ground. Cathryn's screams turned into dry, heaving sobs as she struggled to draw in breath, and she stumbled backwards, trying to compel her legs to flee, but they remained rooted on the spot. She stared at the monster before her, watching in terror as it slowly turned to look at her. Its eyes were like blazing fires, while the scales on its body gleamed red in the sunlight. Huge red wings spread from its back, and a tail of sharp spears swished back and forth over the ground, swirling up eddies of dust. The sobs caught in her throat as the blazing eyes of the beast held hers. A movement caught her eye, and she glanced over to see Geoffrey getting to his feet and slowly backing away.

"I've heard dragons only eat pretty maidens," he said with a nervous laugh, "so I'll just leave you to it."

With a roar the dragon pounced, a stream of flame pouring from its mouth as it pinned Geoffrey to the ground with its sharp talons, its lips drawn back in a snarl.

"No," shouted Cathryn, "don't eat him." The dragon turned to look at her once more, and if she hadn't known better she could have sworn he was looking at her in disbelief. She took a deep swallow. "I think you will find his flesh stringy and his flavor as putrid as his heart."

The dragon watched her for another moment before slowly, and with obvious reluctance, pulling its claws away, leaving Geoffrey free to scramble to his feet. With an angry look at Cathryn, he turned and walked away, pushing through the hedge and disappearing from sight. Cathryn watched him go, before turning back to look at the dragon.

"Thank you," she whispered. The creature nodded, and she turned around, running back down the path.

"Cathryn." A breath of warm air swept over her as she

heard her name whispered, but she didn't pause, and didn't look back.

CHAPTER TWENTY-TWO

When Cathryn returned to the inn, Geoffrey was waiting in the front parlor. He approached her as soon as she entered the building, and when she deliberately turned her back to him and walked away he grabbed her arm.

"Please, Cathryn," he pleaded, "let me apologize."

"What for?" she asked, turning around to face him. "Trying to force yourself on me, or offering me to the dragon?"

"For both," he replied. "I should never have forced my attentions on you, despite the fact that we are to be married. I'm afraid I allowed my amorous desires to get the better of me." Cathryn snorted, but he was already continuing. "And I never intended for you to be eaten by the dragon — I was merely creating a distraction so that you could get away."

Cathryn stared at him for a moment, eyebrows raised incredulously, before giving a humorless laugh.

"Is that the best you can do?" she asked.

"Please Cathryn," he implored, "allow me to prove my sincerity."

Taking a step back, she shook off his hand.

"Do not ever lay your hands on me again," she said, her

voice low and hard.

"Everything all right, Mistress?" At the sound of Felix's voice, Cathryn glanced around to see him standing a few feet away. His eyes were narrowed as he looked at Geoffrey, but softened when they turned to her.

"Thank you, Felix," she said, forcing a smile. "Everything is fine."

With her chin in the air, Cathryn swept out of the room without another glance at Geoffrey, but on reaching her room, she slumped down against the door. Her hair fell across her face, and she remembered the hairpin, lying fallen in the dirt in the field. Suddenly it all seemed too much to bear, and she buried her head in her hands as a sudden headache overwhelmed her. She sat like that for a few minutes, but then pushed herself back to her feet and crossed over to the window. Her room looked down the lane she had walked with Geoffrey, the small stone church at the end. Beyond the church she could see the open fields, but the dragon was no longer there. She stared at the spot where the beast had been, sure that even if she could not see him, the creature was close by, watching over her.

It was suppertime when Cathryn finally ventured from her room. As she headed down the stairs, she could hear Geoffrey's voice ringing out in laughter, and as she stepped into the dining hall, he quickly made his way to her side.

"Come sit with me," he said with a charming smile.

"I would prefer to sit on my own," she replied.

"Come, Cathryn," he cajoled, "give me a chance to redeem myself. You know that I have the utmost respect for you."

"Was it respect for me that made you treat me like a wench from a bawdyhouse?" she asked with scorn. "Is that the reason you offered me to the dragon?"

"I did allow my desire for you to go a bit far," he said with a sheepish grin, "and you know I would never have let the dragon eat you. I just thought that with the dragon's attention on me, you would have a chance to escape."

"Ah," she replied. "So you were offering yourself!"

"Exactly," he replied.

Cathryn looked at him with a mixture of amusement and scorn.

"Very well, find us a table," she said.

The meal was a hearty stew, and Cathryn felt herself reviving as she ate. As soon as she was done, she excused herself and made her way back to her room, waving at Hannah to stay when she made a move to follow. The room was cool, and she walked over to the window to pull the shutters closed. She held a candle in her hand, and it shone unsteadily around the room, catching objects for a moment and then flickering away again. Something glittered on her bed, and she turned to see what it was, gasping when she saw the butterfly pin resting on top of the quilts. Her gaze flew around the room and then settled on the open shutters. Placing the candle on the bed stand, she walked over to the open window. Beyond the lights of the inn the night was dark, but in the darkness glowed two small flames. His name formed on her lips, but she pressed them tight, squashing the word as she pulled the shutters closed.

CHAPTER TWENTY-THREE

The next few days offered little possibility of peace and respite. A morning spent inspecting fleeces at market was followed by traveling over the countryside to the next estate, reaching it just as the sun was about to set. Contracts were reviewed and negotiations conducted by candlelight, allowing for the fleeces to be loaded onto wagons at first light and the entourage to set off once more, towards the next destination. Cathryn had expected Geoffrey to return to town after her refusal of an immediate marriage, but he was not deterred. Instead, he traveled with the convoy, using what opportunity he had to further his case for an immediate marriage.

"I really do not understand your reluctance to finalize the contract," he complained one day.

"And I do not understand your desire for haste," she retorted.

"My dear Cathryn," he replied, "it is because I find your company so enchanting. I long to know that I will have you forever by my side."

There was another creature that seemed determined to make its presence felt, striking fear into the hearts of the convoy. Every day the dragon could be seen circling the sky above them, its huge wings casting shadows on the ground below. It was close enough that Cathryn could have looked it straight in the eye, but apart from a quick glance every once in a while, she studiously ignored the creature. The guards and wagoners had slowly grown used to the beast circling above them, when it became clear that it intended them no harm, and they tolerated the beast with little complaining.

Despite her best intentions to ignore the creature flying above, the presence of the dragon allowed Cathryn no peace. Every fiber in her body seemed attuned to its presence. She knew when it was close, and when it flew into the distance. She watched the horizon when it disappeared for a short time, quickly turning away when it reappeared. Her heart pounded when she felt the beating of its wings stirring the air around her, and her neck prickled when she felt the warmth of its flames. Every night she stood at her window, pushing all thoughts of the beast from her mind, even as she scanned the vista for some sight of it. She refused to call it by name in her thoughts, but felt the blood rush to her cheeks when she thought of it flying above her.

Four days went by before the entourage entered another town. As they approached, Cathryn noticed the dragon veer away from the small habitation, dropping behind some trees not too far away. It didn't take long for the party to find an inn to accommodate them, and Cathryn slipped out of the saddle gratefully, struggling to keep her balance when her legs would have given way. She stood in the sunlight for a moment, considering the shabby building ahead of her, before turning on her heel and walking away. She had no thought in mind beyond a desire to stretch her legs, but after a few minutes found herself entering a small copse of trees. Although it was shady, the air was warm, and she twisted her way around the trunks, enjoying the peace and quiet. She could see an area of sunlight up ahead, and she moved towards it, but the sight that met her eyes brought her to a sudden standstill. Ahead of her, facing the opposite direction, lay the dragon. From where she stood, she could see its enormous tail resting on the ground, armed with sharp spikes. Its wings, folded on its back, shimmered in the sunlight, and a sharp ridge of bone ran along its back, extending into the spikes on its tail and creating more spikes down its neck. She pulled in a breath, and carefully took a step backwards, but the sound of the dragon's voice froze her in place.

"I know you are there," he said gently. "Please don't run away." Slowly the dragon lifted his head, and stretching his long neck, turned to look at her, taking in a deep breath as he did so. "You're scared of me," he said, his voice low. "I won't hurt you."

"You're a dragon," she whispered, nervousness making her voice high.

"I am many things," he said, "and a dragon is just one of them."

"How can you say that? You're a … you're a monster."

"No," he whispered. "I may be a beast, but I am not a monster."

Cathryn dropped her eyes, taking another step backwards.

"Please," he said, "don't go. Stay for a little while. I won't hurt you. I could never hurt you."

"You already have," said Cathryn, so softly it was little more than a breath. But she shifted her feet, moving slightly forward. Watching her carefully, the dragon slowly turned his body around so that he faced her. He brought his massive head down to Cathryn's eye level, but stayed a few yards back. Cathryn could see the horns that rose from his skull, sharp and dangerous, while his nostrils flared at the end of a long snout, and she could see the row upon row of wickedly sharp teeth that lined his mouth. At his full height the creature would tower over her, but he lay crouched, close to the ground.

"I'm sorry I hurt you," said the dragon. "Would it have made a difference if I told you?"

Cathryn looked at the creature for a long time, before closing her eyes.

"No," she whispered.

"Cathryn," said the dragon, his voice pained.

"I think I should go," she said, turning away.

"How can you find it in your heart to forgive Geoffrey Beaumont for acting as he did, but you cannot forgive me for being who I am?"

"Because," Cathryn said, turning around again and taking a step closer, "he is a man, a human, and my future husband." With a growl the dragon leaned forward, bringing his head closer to hers as she took a quick step back.

"I think," he said, sparks flying from his nostrils, "you are mistaking the monster."

"The monster stands right in front of me," she retorted, her voice rising.

"You refuse to look beyond the outward appearance," he said. "It is not what you see on the outside that matters, but what is within. There is nothing within Geoffrey Beaumont that you could possibly admire. Or perhaps I have misjudged you, and you are as shallow as he is."

"How dare you?" she said, her voice growing louder as she took another step towards the dragon.

"How dare I?" he growled back, lifting his head as he glared down at her, his eyes flaming. "You are the one turning your back on everything important for the sake of outward appearances."

"Appearances," she scoffed. "There is more at stake here than appearances. You are an animal!"

"You think humans are better than animals?" he asked, his voice dropping low. "Just look at the way humans treat each other — they kill and maim. They torture and starve one another. They are no better than the wildest beast in the fields. Worse, because they know what they are doing."

"And you don't?" she said. "When you attack and kill, do you not know what you are doing?"

"You are judging me based on what you have heard in stories," he said, his tone harsh. "You think who I am changes because I take on a different form? That is all it is, Cathryn, a different form. I am not the monster you hear about in the tales."

"Then who are you?" she demanded. The dragon dropped its head to her level once more, bringing its face within a foot of hers.

"Why don't you find out?" he said softly. Cathryn stared at its flaming eyes for a moment, before turning around and walking away without another word.

That night as she lay in bed, Cathryn thought about the challenge in the dragon's words. Did she want to find out what the dragon was like? And would it even make a difference? She still did not have an answer when she finally fell into a fitful sleep.

The party set off early again the next morning. Only half of the wagons remained; the others, overflowing with fleeces, were sent back to town where the goods would be stored in the warehouse. With a smaller convoy, the pace picked up a little and Cathryn was eager to make the next town that day. She did not relish the thought of sleeping under the stars.

They had barely left the town gates when the dragon appeared in the sky again, swooping down low over them. As he circled around, he drew close to Cathryn on her mount, turning his head to look directly at her. Reluctantly, she turned her face to look at him, meeting the blazing gaze of the beast before he straightened his neck and arced his way up into the heavens. As Cathryn watched him go, she had to admit that he was a creature of beauty. The sun glinted off the red scales, burnishing them with light, while the silky wings glittered as they cleaved through the air. An errant thought made Cathryn wonder whether they would be soft to touch, before she put it aside in annoyance. She would not, she determined, give the creature another single thought.

CHAPTER TWENTY-FOUR

A week went by before Cathryn found her resolve breaking, and she headed for the field where she had seen the dragon land earlier in the day as they had entered the next town. She walked slowly, fearful of startling the beast, but as she approached the field, she could see the creature already watching her approach with an air of expectancy. She stopped, meeting his fiery gaze before allowing her eyes to slide over the rest of his huge form, noting the shiny scales, sharp barbs, deadly horns and silky wings. She walked forward a little more, but stopped when she was about ten feet away.

"Do you regret being a dragon?" she asked. The bony ridge above the dragon's eyes rose as he looked at her in surprise.

"No, of course not. This is what I am. I was born a dragon. Do you wish you were something other than human?"

"Well, no, but then I don't hunt down people and eat them."

"Nor do I," he replied. "My diet does not differ that much from yours. While you may not be out in the forest with bow and arrow, you enjoy the labors of other hunters."

"But you don't use a bow and arrow!"

"Cathryn, are you objecting to my method of hunting? We are all limited by our natures and physical abilities — humans, dragons, even the wolf and lynx."

Cathryn was silent. Pulling a leaf from a tree, she fiddled with it while the dragon watched.

"What's wrong?" he finally asked. Cathryn looked up at him, catching her breath when she saw he had moved closer.

"I haven't had a wolf ask me to marry him," she snapped. The dragon lifted his head and laughed, flames streaming from his mouth as he did so, while Cathryn glared at him in silence.

"Oh, my love," he said at last, dropping his head low once more as Cathryn took a step back.

"Don't call me that," she said sharply.

"Why not?" he asked. "It is what you are."

"What does a dragon know about love?"

"You think a dragon cannot love?" he said. "Cathryn, this is getting tedious. You have a very fixed idea of who and what I am, and you will not admit to anything that contradicts your beliefs."

"Why do you keep this form?" she demanded, waving her hand through the air in his direction. The dragon regarded her in silence for a moment before slowly responding.

"Seeing me like this scares you, doesn't it? You cannot see past the monster you have heard about in the tales. You think I am going to hurt you." He watched her closely, and Cathryn looked away, refusing to meet his penetrating gaze.

"You didn't answer my question," she finally said.

"The answer is, because I do not wish to offend your sense of propriety."

Cathryn looked back at him in surprise.

"My sense of propriety?"

"Yes. As you can see, I travel light. I do not have a change of clothes."

"Oh!" Cathryn turned around to hide the color rising in her cheeks. She took a deep breath and turned to face him once more. "I suppose that is a reasonable explanation."

"I certainly think so. But the problem still remains that my current form terrifies you." He cocked his head as he looked at her. "Come closer," he said.

"Why?"

"Come touch the monster," he said, dropping his voice.

"I'm not scared of you," she said, taking a step forward.

"Closer," he said. She closed her eyes for a moment, drawing in deeply to control her trembling, before taking another step forward. Slowly, cautiously, the dragon stretched his long neck towards her, until he was a few mere inches away. He looked at Cathryn, holding her gaze as she slowly lifted a hand to the side of his neck. She could feel the heat coming from him, like a raging fire, and she paused for a moment. Stretching out her fingers, she touched the heated surface, sliding her fingers over the glossy scales. She had never felt anything so smooth, and where the scales joined, they slipped from one to another with barely a ripple. The breath caught in her throat, and she dropped her hand, taking a step back once more. The dragon looked at her carefully, dropping his head so that she could see the top of his skull. The treacherous horns, reaching to the sky, gleamed in the sun, and Cathryn could feel the fear rising once more.

"Trust me," he whispered, dropping his head further. "I am not a wild beast, easily startled. I am the one who loves you, and would forever hold you safe."

Slowly, tentatively, she reached towards the horns. The movement made her skirts rustle over his face, but he made no move. She could sense the tension in his massive body as he held himself taut, waiting for her to touch him, and she stroked her hand over the hard surface, running her thumb up and over the rounded point of the horn. It was solid, but like the rest of him was warm. She dropped her hand and let it slide over the top of his skull as she gently pulled back. A slight shudder ran through him, and she drew away in fright, her heart suddenly racing. They eyed each other in silence, but slowly Cathryn felt the fear dissipate, and she gave him a tentative smile.

"Cathryn," he said, "this monster has a name. Please say it."

"You're not a monster," she said. He smiled, a huge toothy smile.

"Say my name."

Cathryn looked away as she whispered under her breath. "Favian."

"Look at me," he said softly. Slowly she turned to look at him, meeting his blazing gaze. "Say it again," he said.

"Favian," she said, her eyes caught by his. "Your name is Favian."

"Cathryn," he paused. "I love you."

She dropped her gaze and took a step backwards. "I have to go," she said.

"I will see you tomorrow," he said. She nodded, turning away.

It was a mild evening, and as she approached the inn, Cathryn could see people milling around the old building, some of them loud and raucous. She paused for a moment as she looked for the best route through the crowd, when a figure broke away and strode towards her.

"Geoffrey," she said.

"What are you doing out here?" he asked.

"Just taking a walk," she replied, taking a step towards the building.

"A walk? At night? By yourself?" he said, turning to follow her.

"Yes," she replied, hastening her step.

"Maybe you were meeting someone?" he said. Cathryn stopped, turning around to face him. Did he mean the dragon? "Got a lover, have you? Felix perhaps?"

Cathryn stared at him incredulously.

"You have gone mad," she said with a dry laugh. "Now goodnight."

"Not so fast," he said, grabbing her arm. "You are my future wife, and I insist you tell me where you have been."

"Can I make the same demands of you when you are off sneaking around?" she demanded. "If you must know, I went to see the dragon." He dropped her arm and stepped back, his eyes narrowed.

"You went to see the dragon? That sounds like a likely story. Why would you do that?"

"Perhaps I find the company of the dragon preferable to any I might find around here," she retorted. "Now let me pass. I am going to bed. Alone. With the door bolted and barred."

CHAPTER TWENTY-FIVE

The next night Cathryn and her entourage were the guests of Oliver Calder, a wealthy wine merchant. Felix had told her that the term 'wine merchant' was to be used loosely when it came to their host.

"'Smuggler' would be far more apt," he had said, tapping the side of his nose to show that this was a well-known secret. Cathryn had smiled to herself; and tonight, when her host offered her a glass of fine French wine at supper, she bent her head to hide her smile. The hours after the meal were spent closeted in his study as they discussed the terms of the contract, but when they were done, Master Calder offered her another glass of wine before settling back in his chair. *A good-looking man, despite his years,* Cathryn thought as she watched him over the rim of her wineglass. His brown eyes sparkled as he returned her regard.

"I understand you are traveling with a dragon," he said, and Cathryn sucked a mouthful of wine into her lungs. Groping for the desk, she replaced the cup and leaned over as she coughed. Her host was up in a moment, pounding her on the back.

"Are you all right, my dear?" he asked as she regained

her breath. Her eyes were watering, and she could feel the heat in her cheeks.

"Fine," she managed. Master Calder returned to his seat, and poured himself another glass.

"So," he said when she was finally breathing normally, "the dragon."

"Well," she said, "we are not actually traveling with the dragon. It is more that he is traveling with us. Following us, I mean," she added hastily.

"He?" the man prodded gently.

"Um ... it," she said, looking down at her hands. She waited for him to continue, looking up when he didn't. He was regarding her with a peculiar expression, but it vanished when he met her gaze.

"Fearful monsters, dragons," he said. "I've heard horrible stories of how they eat, pillage and burn."

"Hmm," she said, waving her hand vaguely. "I wouldn't really know."

"Wouldn't you? I thought maybe you did," he said.

"I really don't know much about dragons," she repeated. "That ... creature ... keeps following us, and we have grown accustomed to its presence, especially since it has not tried to harm us, but beyond that I know nothing about dragons, or why this one has kept us in its sights. Now if you will excuse me, I should bid you good night."

"Before you go," he said, holding up a hand to forestall her departure, "I was just wondering about something. I happen to know some people who live in your part of the country — perhaps you know them? Name of Drake. Favian Drake." Cathryn had started rising from her seat, but at his words she felt her legs give way beneath her and she fell back into the seat with a graceless thump.

"Favian Drake?" she said, her voice unsteady. "I don't believe I know that name." She glanced up to meet his gaze before hurriedly looking away again.

"What a pity," he said. "I received word that Favian

Drake was in the vicinity, so I sent a note inviting him to join us on the morrow. I thought perhaps it would be comforting to see a face from home, but since you don't know the man …" He waved a hand to dismiss the subject.

"No," she said, "I'm afraid I don't." She pushed herself to her feet again, holding the desk to steady herself, before nodding at her host. "Goodnight."

Cathryn took her time the next morning, changing her gown twice and insisting Hannah redo her hair, until the maid fairly pushed her from the room.

"You look fine, Mistress," she said. "Master Calder will be waiting for you."

She left the room and slowly walked towards the hall, Hannah close on her heels. As she entered the room, Master Calder waved from a table on the dais at the far end.

"Mistress Cathryn," he shouted, making his voice heard above the hubbub. The seat next to him was empty, and he indicated it with his hand. Cathryn responded with a nod, her heart sinking as she saw the person seated to the other side of the empty chair, his eyes watching her carefully as his gaze met hers. She heard Hannah gasp behind her, and Cathryn dropped her gaze as she slowly made her way along the length of the hall and up to the table.

"Mistress Cathryn," Master Calder said, standing and making a slight bow. "Allow me to introduce Favian Drake. As I mentioned last night, he lives in your corner of the world."

"Master Drake." Cathryn gave him a quick glance before looking away.

"Mistress Cathryn," he said. He had stood at her approach, and now waved a hand in the direction of the empty seat. "Please, won't you sit down?"

Cathryn nodded, and moved around the table, catching Geoffrey's glare; he was seated on the opposite end next to Felix.

"I trust you had a good night's rest," Master Calder said as she took her seat. It took Cathryn a moment to register what he was saying.

"Uh, yes, thank you," she assured her host. "I passed a very comfortable night." It was a lie, of course, but he seemed satisfied. Next to her, Cathryn could feel the heat rising from Favian's skin. *He is too close*, she thought. He adjusted his seat slightly, and she felt her heart speed up when his leg brushed against hers.

"What are you doing here?" she hissed at him.

"Visiting a friend," he whispered as he leaned past her to grab the wine. "I hear you are still denying all knowledge of me. I thought we had moved beyond that."

"You are incorrigible," she said.

"Yes, so you have said before."

Favian was so close to her she could feel his breath drifting over her. He brushed against her whenever he reached for something on the table, making her every nerve strain towards him.

"You cannot escape me," he whispered when she tried to move away. "I will pursue you to the ends of the earth." She turned to look at him, the breath catching in her throat when his gaze caught hers.

She pushed herself away from the table as soon as she could without being rude, and quickly weaved her way back through the room. Out of the corner of her eye she saw Hannah watching her quizzically, and she groaned inwardly as she left the hall. She was striding quickly toward her chambers when the sound of footsteps in the passage behind her made her slow down, and she turned to see Favian close on her heels.

"Cathryn," he said softly, approaching her with caution, "the main reason I am here is that I wanted to see you. Like this." He waved his hands over his form.

"Oh," she whispered. Another step brought him close enough to touch, and he looked down at her, his eyes

135

glowing with the faint sparks of yellow she had seen before. "Do your eyes ever turn to flames when you are like this?" she asked. He took another step closer and took her hands in his, looking down at them as he gently stroked them. When he looked up again his eyes were burning, yellow and orange flames leaping within them. "Oh," she said again. Lifting his hand, he trailed his fingers down her cheek, before cupping her face in his hands.

"Every time I see you I want to touch you like this," he whispered. "You have been so afraid of me. Please tell me that you are no longer fearful." She looked at him, mesmerized by his eyes, before dragging her gaze away.

"How do you know Master Calder?" she asked. Favian sighed, dropping his hands from her face.

"He's a good friend of the family, and a ..." He paused. "We are distantly related," he finally finished.

"Related?" she asked softly.

"Yes."

"Then is he ...? Does that mean ...?" Her words trailed off.

"Yes," he said. "Oliver Calder is also a monster."

"Don't say that," she said sharply.

"Why not? It is what you think, is it not?"

"No! Argh, I don't know any more." She turned from him with a groan. "Life was so simple before you came along."

"Simple, perhaps." She could hear the amusement in his tone. "But so dreadfully dull and boring." He pulled away as other footsteps sounded along the passage. "It is my understanding that you will remain here for another night, and Oliver has invited me to stay as his guest, so I will see you around the estate." The footsteps drew closer. "Mistress," he said. She turned to see him give a shallow bow before turning away and disappearing down the passage. Picking up her skirts, she hurried down the passage towards her own chambers, her mind in turmoil.

The remainder of the day was spent at a makeshift table, meeting with the tenant farmers who kept flocks on the estate. With more than five thousand fleeces between them, it made for a busy afternoon. Felix helped her inspect the fleeces as she made notes in a large ledger, while the wagoners tied them into bundles and hauled them onto the wagons. She saw Geoffrey watching her for a while, before he left and walked in the direction of the stable. She could not understand why he was still traveling with them, and she watched his retreating figure in puzzlement. A peripheral movement caught her eye and she turned to see Favian watching her. She felt her cheeks flush as she returned her attention to the ledger before her.

The sun was already low on the horizon when Cathryn finally slammed the ledger closed. Her hand was stiff, her legs were numb and her back was sore. There was a small pond surrounded by trees at the front of the house, and handing the ledger over to Felix, she headed in that direction. As she rounded the corner of the house, she saw Favian and Oliver standing near the pond. She drew back slightly, watching as Favian ran his hands through his hair in a gesture of frustration, shaking his head at something the other man had said. He stared at the pond as the other man continued speaking, leaning earnestly towards Favian. Once again Favian shook his head. As Cathryn watched, a slight breeze stirred the air, and she saw the two men stop their conversation as they both lifted their heads. Slowly Favian turned to peer into the shadows where Cathryn stood, and she pulled herself further towards the house, until the sound of footsteps on the gravel path behind her made her spin around. She groaned to herself when she saw who it was.

"Cathryn," said Geoffrey, coming up to her, "how does Favian Drake come to be a guest of Calder?"

"I'm afraid I am not privy to the man's personal affairs," she replied. She glanced back towards the pond, turning in that direction when she saw that the other men had gone. "I barely know the man," she said.

"He was watching you," said Geoffrey.

"What exactly are you accusing me of?" she said, turning around to face him.

"I would just like to know the nature of your relationship with him," he replied.

"Relationship!" said Cathryn, her voice rising in pitch. "There is no relationship between me and Favian Drake. I barely know him! He means nothing to me."

"Mistress Cathryn." Cathryn whirled around at the voice behind her, her face paling as she saw Favian. His face was expressionless, but his eyes were dark, the color of stormy waters. She raised her hand to her mouth as she caught her breath, horrified at what he must have heard.

"Favian," she whispered under her breath, "I'm sorry." She could feel the tears gathering in her eyes, and picking up her skirts, she pushed past him and ran towards the house.

Hannah came to the room a short while later.

"Please tell Master Calder that I have a headache and won't be able to join him for supper," Cathryn said.

Hannah sat down on the bed beside Cathryn. "Does this have something to do with Favian Drake being here? Because it is not like you to run away."

"I know," she groaned, "but I just cannot face him. Please Hannah, just give my apologies."

Hannah nodded and left the room, leaving Cathryn to her thoughts. She stood at the window, listening to the cheerful clamor that came from below as the meal was served. She pulled out her notes, then pushed them away again in frustration, unable to focus on the words on the sheet. Stars began to appear in the darkening sky, and she lay on the bed, but when sleep refused to come, she rose once more and paced the room. She heard the house growing quieter, but she was unable to still her agitated mind. She listened as the house settled, eventually falling into silence, before she carefully opened her door and listened once more. Assured that all was quiet, she crept down the stairs, heading towards the study she was in the previous night. There had been a few books in there, she recalled, and she didn't think her host would begrudge her borrowing one.

The door to the room was open and she slipped in quietly, lifting the candle she had brought with her as she sought out the books. A slight noise in the corner of the room had her swinging the candle around in fright, but it was only a mouse scurrying along the length of the wall. She sighed in relief, turning back towards the shelves, when she felt the hairs at the back of her neck rise. Taking in a deep breath, she turned around slowly, holding the candle high again. The single flame did little to disperse the darkness, and she moved forward slowly, holding the light before her. Suddenly, a flame flared ahead of her, illuminating the room, and she staggered backwards, hitting her hip against the desk, as Favian stood before her, a flame burning in the palm of his hand. She stared at it in horror, only looking up at him when he closed his fist around the blaze. Flames leaped within his eyes, and he watched her intently as he stalked closer, taking the listing candle from her hand and placing it on the desk.

He lifted his hand to her face and trailed his fingers down her cheek and across her lips, and then his mouth was on hers, hard and demanding. His tongue invaded her mouth, and she felt her traitorous body respond to his. Her hands reached up his neck, pushing into the hair pulled back with a ribbon. His kiss gentled but delved even deeper, and she could feel the heat starting in her belly and spreading through her limbs. He pulled away from her mouth, and trailed kisses down her neck and onto her shoulders, before returning his lips to hers. She moaned into his mouth, and he pulled away, panting. His forehead dropped to hers and she heard him groan her name, his fingers caressing her back and neck. His breath steadied and he pulled away, looking at her with eyes burning bright.

"Does this feel like 'nothing', Cathryn?" he whispered. "Can you really say you feel nothing for me?"

"Favian," she said, trying to pull away, but his arms gave her no freedom of movement. "I'm sorry," she whispered. "I did not know what to say."

"How about the truth, Cathryn? You are making both of us miserable by your continual refusal to face the truth."

"I don't know what the truth is," she said, finally freeing herself from his grasp and turning away.

"Yes, you do," he said. "Almost from the first time you met me you have known the truth, but you keep denying it."

"And what is the truth?" she demanded.

"The truth is that we belong together, Cathryn. We are two sides of a coin, and without the other, neither one of us will be whole."

"No," she said, "you are a dragon."

"Yes," he said with exasperation, "and what of it? My father is a dragon too." Cathryn looked at him in confusion. "My mother is human," he explained. Cathryn pulled back in surprise.

"She is? But how is that possible?"

"Cathryn, only a human woman can bear a dragon child."

"But ... I don't understand."

"It is the nature of dragons. Dragon woman are unable to bear children."

"So you need me for my breeding ability?"

Favian glared at her in exasperation.

"Have I not made myself clear?" he growled. "If all I needed was someone to breed with, well, there are many candidates. I love you, Cathryn, and want to spend the remainder of my life with you."

"No," she whispered.

"No?" he repeated incredulously.

"I mean," Cathryn said, "I cannot give you an answer." She turned around and paced towards the window. "I cannot think!"

"There is nothing to think about," he said, coming up behind her. "Just listen to your heart."

She knew what her heart was saying, but how could she blindly follow it into the dragon's den? She turned to face him.

"I need to go," she said.

"Cathryn, don't deny what your heart is telling you. You know the truth of what I am saying." He sighed when she didn't respond. "When we leave tomorrow," he said, "I won't be like this." He waved a hand over his body.

She nodded. "Leave your clothes in my saddle bag," she said. "I will keep them for you."

"I'll take that as a promise," he said with a smile, "that I will see you again." Dropping his lips to hers, he kissed her gently, before pulling back and allowing her to pass.

CHAPTER TWENTY-SIX

Cathryn was up early the next morning, eager to get on the road before the sun was too far above the horizon. She entered the warm and noisy hall, where the men in her retinue were pulling on boots and leather jerkins. Calder had ordered food to be ready for them to take and enjoy on the road, and hunks of warm, yeasty bread lay on the table. As she picked her way through the men, Cathryn spotted Oliver Calder watching her closely. He smiled when she met his gaze, and made his way towards her.

"I'm afraid my other guest had to leave even earlier than you this morning," he said.

"Your other guest?" she said, proud at the even tone of her voice. "Oh, you mean Master, eh, Drake."

"Well done," said Oliver with a grin, but she kept her expression bland. "He left at first light, but I'm sure you will see him again soon." He gave her a sly wink before leaning towards her, his tone suddenly serious. "Look to the heart, Mistress Cathryn, when judging a person's character. That is where you will see the truth of an individual." Cathryn stared at him as he took a step back, giving her a shallow bow before turning away.

Cathryn grabbed a hunk of bread and headed out the hall towards the stables, where the stable boy was tightening the straps under Morana's belly. Opening the saddle bag, she glanced inside as she packed the bread. Favian's tunic and breeches had been placed at the bottom, and Cathryn reached in to stroke the fabric. The scent of Favian rose to her nose, and she closed her eyes for a brief moment, remembering the way he had kissed her the night before. She felt a flare of heat rush through her at the memory, before opening her eyes and pulling the saddle bag closed. A glint of light made her pause, and she lifted the cover again to peer back inside. Something red sparkled against the fabric of Favian's clothes, and wrapping her fingers around it, Cathryn carefully pulled it into the sunlight. From a chain of silver hung a pendant the size of a large coin. The center of the pendant was a bright, shiny red, and turning it over, Cathryn could see that it was very thin and light. The whole piece had been edged in silver, and it lay warm in her hands. It took a moment for her to realize what it was she was looking at; but when she did, she gasped, for lying in her palm was the scale of a dragon. It glinted in her hands, and she stroked her thumb over the smooth surface, remembering how his scales had felt beneath her hand. Lifting the chain around her neck, she secured the clasp. She could feel the warmth of the scale as it settled on her chest, gleaming against the fabric of her gown.

The convoy of travelers had grown smaller over the weeks, which made for faster progress, but even so it was late when the group reached the next town, and after a brief dinner and an even briefer consultation with Felix, Cathryn collapsed into the hard, lumpy bed of yet another wayside inn and quickly fell asleep.

They were on the road early again the next morning, and by the end of the day Cathryn felt she had reason to be satisfied. Not only had they met with the owner of another large estate with whom she had not previously done business, but she had also reached the next town while the sun was still above the horizon. With only two more estates to visit, Cathryn felt like her time on the road was almost at an end. The fair spring weeks were starting to give way to the heat of summer, and although the hard baked roads were easier to travel, it also meant days spent in the sun.

Cathryn glanced up at the sky, watching the dragon as it flew through the air above her. She knew a decision needed to be made, but why did the man she loved have to be a wild monster?

The dragon had dropped below a small hill covered in trees, and after wetting her palate with a glass of wine, Cathryn made her way in that direction, stopping first to grab Favian's clothes from her saddle bag. She made quick progress through the trees, pausing at the summit of a small hillock to look down at the clearing below where the large, red dragon lay, his eyes fixed on her. She smiled and headed down the slope, grabbing onto the tree trunks as her steps hastened towards the beast. She had just reached the edge of the clearing when the dragon leaped forward with a snarl, and Cathryn fell back with a look of shock.

"Favian?"

"Geoffrey has followed you. Quick, hide the clothes." With a sigh of relief, she quickly did as she was bade, pushing the clothes under a small bush before moving to stand next to the creature.

"You were scared of me," he said, his eyes on the trees in front of him.

"Well, yes, but you did snarl at me."

"Not at you, my love. Never at you. That snarl was intended for Geoffrey." He turned to look at her, dropping his gaze to the pendant around her neck. "You carry a part of me when you wear that," he said softly.

"I know." She lifted her hand to it, feeling the warmth of the scale against her skin.

The sound of heavy footsteps broke upon them as Geoffrey suddenly appeared through the trees. At the sight of the dragon, he paused, before turning his attention to Cathryn.

"Geoffrey," she said. "You followed me. Why?"

"I wanted to see if you were meeting a secret lover?"

"Felix?" she demanded. He shook his head.

"No, I quickly realized how foolish it was to think it could be Felix."

"Really? This entire line of thinking is foolish, Geoffrey." Beside her Cathryn could feel the dragon shift restlessly, and Geoffrey gave it a quick, nervous glance, before looking at Cathryn again.

"No, I don't believe it is. I gave it some further thought, and realized there was only one person that you would be meeting."

"Oh, and who is that? The innkeeper?"

"No. Favian Drake." Cathryn felt the color drain from her face as she stared at Geoffrey. Beside her the dragon turned to look at her, but she refused to meet his gaze.

"Favian Drake?" she faltered. "How do you come to that conclusion?"

"I think he went to the Calder Estate to meet you, and has been following us, unnoticed on the road."

"That's ridiculous!"

"Is it? I have seen the way he watches you, and the way you carefully avoid looking at him. Admit it. You've been meeting him, whoring yourself at every opportunity."

"How dare you?" she cried, but her words were swallowed by the roar that sounded from the dragon as flames spewed from his mouth. Before Cathryn could even register what was happening, the dragon was in the air, Geoffrey clasped in his talons.

"No," Cathryn shouted. "Let him go!" The air around her pulsed at the beat of the dragon's wings as he paused in the air, before slowly twisting his neck and glaring down at

145

her. "Let him go," she said again. "This is my fight, not yours." The dragon shook his head, turning back towards the sky. "Please," she whispered. With a sigh of flame, the dragon opened his claws, releasing Geoffrey from his grasp. Screaming as he fell, Geoffrey landed with a heavy thud, and Cathryn winced as she heard a bone snap. She watched dispassionately as Geoffrey slowly pushed himself up from the ground, grimacing as he straightened his leg.

"Help me up," he groaned.

"No," she said. "This is your own doing. You were very rude."

"Unconscionably rude," he agreed, "even if it was true." He grimaced again as he straightened himself, dragging himself over to a tree where he leaned his weight. "I didn't realize your pet dragon was so protective." He glanced up, but the dragon in question was no longer in sight. "Please don't bring him into my house after we are married," he said. Cathryn gave a dry, humorless laugh.

"What makes you think I still want to marry you?"

"Why wouldn't you?" he asked, a look of surprise crossing his features.

"Because you are the most self-serving person I have ever met," she retorted.

"Ah," he said, with a pained grin, "but what serves my interests also serves yours. Besides, we do have a written agreement." He placed his broken leg on the ground, tentatively testing his weight before grimacing once more.

"Agreements can be broken," she said, watching him.

"But what would that serve?" he asked, glancing at her. "Have your little affairs, by all means, but keep them discreet, and do not — ever — try and keep knowledge of them from me."

"Tell me," she said, her eyes narrowing, "do you see Favian Drake waiting to meet me?"

"No," he replied, "it appears I was incorrect about the reason for your assignation this evening. You were checking on your pet."

"You are wrong about my relationship with Favian Drake. I have never slept with him."

"No? Well then, my apologies for the slur upon your character. Now are you going to help me back to the inn or not?"

"No," she replied. "You got yourself into this trouble, and you can get yourself out."

"At least walk with me," he said.

"No," she said, "now go."

His eyes narrowed for a moment. "Is Favian Drake hiding in the trees?"

"Argh! Enough of this! Just go!" She watched as he slowly hobbled away, and when he finally disappeared through the trees, she sat down on a log to await the dragon's return. She peered through the gathering gloom of dusk and saw a shadow high in the sky. It circled around slowly, but made no effort to drop lower. Slipping onto the cold ground, Cathryn leaned her back against the log where she had been sitting, and closed her eyes. She must have fallen asleep, because the next thing she knew it was dark. She glanced around in confusion before her eyes fell on Favian, sitting a few feet away. His face was in shadow, but she could see that he was dressed in the clothes she had brought.

"You came back," she said with a sleepy smile. "I was hoping to see your wings."

Favian smiled, rising to his feet and walking over to her. He reached down a hand and pulled her up, holding her close when she fell against his chest.

"You can still see my wings," he whispered.

"How?" she asked.

"Like this," he said, pulling away from her, and in one swift movement, he pulled the tunic over his head. She gaped at the sight of him standing half-naked before her in the pale moonlight, then gasped when she saw wings spread

147

above his shoulders. With eyes wide, she walked around him, looking at the wings as they spread from his back. They were huge, stretching to points more than ten feet on either side of him. The bottom of the wings trailed on the ground, while the tips stretched up high above his head. They were the most magnificent things she had ever seen.

"Can I touch them?" she whispered.

"Yes," he said, his voice low as he looked over his shoulder at her. She lifted her hand to the smooth surface, running her fingers over the taut membranes which stretched like silk across a bony frame. They quivered slightly at her touch, the movement making the warm air stir around her. She walked along the outside of one wing to the point, before turning around and running her hand along the side facing his back. As she drew near to him, he reached out a hand, and gently wrapped it around her waist, drawing her closer. She looked at him, and his eyes were no longer a deep blue, but were burning flames of yellow and gold. He lifted his other hand and brushed it through her hair, his eyes following the movement before looking back into her eyes. She opened her lips and he claimed them with his own. She twisted herself so her body pressed close to his, while her hands slid up his back, feeling the ridges of bone and sinew that held the weight of his wings. She felt her feet leave the ground as his arms wound around her, and she tangled her feet in his. His wings pulsed through the air as they hovered together a few inches above the ground. The heat from his skin spun around her, caressing her, and she wrapped herself tighter around him. He pulled away from her mouth and buried his face in her hair as she looked over his shoulder, watching the powerful wings move through the air.

"They are so beautiful," she murmured. He pulled away to look at her, a smile on his face.

"Does that mean you are no longer scared of me?"

"Scared of a big, fire-breathing, flesh-eating, spiky-tailed monster like you?" she laughed. "Never!"

"So when are you going to give the news to Geoffrey?" he asked as he gently brought them back to the ground. She looked to him in confusion.

"Why does Geoffrey need to know that I don't fear a dragon?"

"Not that you don't fear the dragon, but that you love the dragon."

"Oh," she said, pulling away and turning around, gazing into the distance. He watched her for a moment.

"You haven't decided to break the contract, have you?" he said.

"Favian ... I ..."

"No," he said, holding up his hand, "do not say anything. I do not wish to hear excuses from you. Even Geoffrey knows you care for me. I heard what he said earlier, about having your little affairs, but let me be very clear — I will not be part of a secret liaison that has me slinking around, unable to acknowledge my love for you. It is all or nothing, Cathryn, and I am starting to think it will be nothing. I have followed you for weeks, waiting patiently for you to come to terms with what I am, but no more. I am leaving. If you have a change of heart, you know where to find me, but I suspect that day will never come." Cathryn turned to stare at him in horror as he strode away from her, but before he had gone very far, he turned on his heel and stalked back to where she was standing, stopping less than a foot away.

"And one more thing, Cathryn, in the interests of total honesty. I told you that we eat the same things, and that is true, but only to a point. I eat human flesh, Cathryn. In fact, I really enjoy it. And you are smelling quite good right now, so you may want to run for your life."

She gasped, stumbling back from him, and then turned on her heel when he laughed, flames pouring from his mouth.

"That's right, Cathryn," he sneered, "run from the monster."

CHAPTER TWENTY-SEVEN

Cathryn did run, but only for a short time before coming to a complete standstill. She could still hear Favian's laugh ringing in her ears, but another voice also whispered at the back of her mind. *Look in the heart and you will see the real character*, she heard Oliver's voice say. No, she thought, Favian is not a monster. She knew him, knew his heart, and knew that despite his angry words he was the man she loved. Perhaps he did eat human flesh, but it was not because he was a monster, hunting down innocent prey, enjoying their terror. Slowly, she turned around and walked back to the clearing, but it was empty.

"Favian," she whispered, but there was no response. "Favian," she said again, raising her voice to a call, and then yelling his name again when there was still no response. His clothes were lying on the ground, and she gathered them into her arms, bringing them to her face to breathe in the smell of him.

He was right, she thought. They were meant to be together, but she had pushed him away, over and over again. He had been patient, and understanding, but she had kept her distance. The red pendant lay upon her chest, and she wrapped her hand around it, feeling the heat of it on her palm.

"Oh, Favian," she whispered. "I am so sorry. I will make this right, I promise." She could feel the tears gathering in her eyes, but she scrubbed them away. Instead of wallowing in self-pity, she needed to take steps to set things to rights. She turned in the direction of the inn, determined to tell Geoffrey that she could not marry him, when a sudden thought brought her to a stop once again. He had tried to force himself on her once, and he could do so again. Perhaps, she decided, this was news better delivered once she was home.

It was dark as she walked back through the trees, but she could see a shimmer of light in the distance and she followed it. It wasn't until she grew closer that she saw the huge branch, pushed into the ground and set alight, a beacon for someone walking in the dark. She stared at it for a long moment before turning around slowly, searching the shadows for signs of a dragon. Or a man. But all around her it was quiet and dark. The light of the blaze fell on the bangle wrapped around her wrist, and slowly she pulled it off, holding it tight in her hands. Favian had given her a part of himself, but all she had to give him in return was a memory. She kissed the bangle before laying it on the ground next to the burning branch. If Favian came back to snuff the torch, then he would find it. And if not ... she shrugged, unwilling to think that he would be that careless.

All was quiet at the inn when she returned, and she carefully made her way through the building and up the stairs to her room, where Hannah was waiting for her.

"You were out late. I was growing worried," she said.

"I ...uh... went for a walk."

"I saw Master Beaumont hobble into the inn. Is everything all right?"

"Yes. He had a run-in with the dragon." She paused. "I cannot marry him."

"Did he hurt you?"

"No."

Hannah watched Cathryn for a moment.

"Did you have a secret assignation with Master Drake?"

Cathryn looked away, her cheeks flushing, but after a moment she turned and met Hannah's gaze.

"Not in the way you mean. But I do intend to marry him."

Cathryn was up at first light the next morning, and after assuring Hannah she would be back soon, she hurried towards the copse of trees, searching the sky for a sign of a dragon. There was none, and with a sigh she turned her attention to the ground. The branch was still planted into the earth, the wood black and cold as it stood starkly against the low morning light, but the bangle was gone.

It was another five days before the little party straggled into town on a warm and sunny afternoon. Geoffrey rode in the wagon, grimacing at every bump and turn, his horse tied to the back. At the sight of her home, Cathryn felt the weariness of the past weeks lift, and she turned to Hannah with a smile.

"Home at last. I'm looking forward to a good meal and a comfortable bed, and I'm sure you are too. Send one of the other maids to my chambers, and then take the rest of the week off."

The clatter of horses and wagon brought Father to the door, and he stepped outside to greet Cathryn.

"Welcome home, daughter," he said, pulling her towards him and giving her a quick peck on the cheek, before dropping his arms and stepping away.

"Father," greeted Cathryn. "You are back. Does that mean you have finished your consultations with the king?"

"No," he replied, "but the court has moved to the summer palace, and the king does not wish to pay attention to matters of state while there are summer balls to enjoy." He shook his head in perturbation. "But enough of that, how goes our wool business?"

"Very well, Father," replied Cathryn, walking past him to enter the house. "I can give you a full report on the morrow, but there is another matter I wish to discuss with you, later this evening after I've had a chance to recover."

"Very well," he said. He watched her for a moment as she mounted the stairs to her chambers, before turning his attention to Felix.

CHAPTER TWENTY-EIGHT

"What?" demanded Father later that evening as they sat in the parlor after supper, his face reddening as he glared at his daughter. "What do you mean, you wish to annul the contract?"

"I love someone else, Father," Cathryn said.

"Love," he scoffed, "what do you know about love? All love does is lead to pain."

Cathryn closed her eyes at her father's words, but then opening them once more, met his gaze unflinchingly. "I would rather experience both love and pain, than live a life feeling nothing at all."

"And who is this man? What makes you think he feels the same for you? Some men are predators, just after money and security."

"He is a good man," she said. "He has no need for my money, and in fact, I would be the one gaining something."

"What would you gain?" he demanded.

"Love, family, a home," she said softly. Father pulled back at her words.

"Cathryn … I may not express it well, but you know I love you."

"I know that, Father," she replied. "But I would like my life to have more meaning than just the business. Favian has helped me to see that there is so much more."

"Favian?"

"Favian Drake," she said.

"Drake ... as in Margaret Drake?"

"Yes," she replied, looking away.

"Ah. You told me you were spending time with your friend."

"And so I was, Father," she retorted. "If you recall, I didn't even want to go, but you insisted upon it. And although Favian was there, he acted as a gentleman the entire duration of my stay."

"I'm sure he did," Father replied dryly. "So you have decided to put your own personal desires above all other considerations. I expected you to be more considerate of your duty to *this* family."

Cathryn looked at him in astonishment. "Everything I have ever done has been for you and the business," she said. "Should my future happiness be laid as a sacrifice on the altar of financial success as well?" She rose to her feet and strode around the room. "A marriage with Geoffrey may tie our respective businesses closer together, but it is not crucial to your success. Indeed, it may prevent you from seeking other partnerships. Or do you want this partnership because it guarantees you the easier path?"

"Cathryn, please ..."

"No," she said. "I am done. I refuse to marry Geoffrey Beaumont. Favian has already offered to make restitution should this result in a financial loss." Father turned to look out the window, his fingers tapping on his leg as Cathryn watched him from behind. After a long moment, he turned to face Cathryn again.

"Very well. If you are determined to follow this path, I will not stand in your way. However, let me just say I am very disappointed."

"Thank you, Father," she said. "I will send a note to Geoffrey on the morrow, asking him to call, and will break the news in person."

Father nodded. "I will be at a guild meeting in the morning. When will I meet this Favian Drake?"

Cathryn looked away.

"I'm ... not sure. Soon."

"Very well," he repeated. "But know this. I will find out all I can about this man, and will not consent to your marriage if I find he is not all you say he is."

"I understand," she said. "Now if you will excuse me, I wish to retire to bed."

"Before you go, Cathryn, Felix has told me that you handled the contracts and negotiations with ease and skill. Well done." He gave her a slight smile. "I look forward to receiving a full report on the morrow. Goodnight."

CHAPTER TWENTY-NINE

Cathryn sent two notes the next morning, asking the recipients to wait upon her. One was addressed to Favian at Drake Manor, the other to Geoffrey Beaumont; the second arrived within half an hour of her note, limping with the aid of a cane.

"Ready to finalize our marriage?" he asked with a grin, carefully making his way into the parlor. "We could go find a priest now if you want."

She poured him a glass of wine and handed it to him, watching while he drank it down. "Actually," she said, taking the glass from him, "I'm not going to marry you, Geoffrey. I want to annul our contract."

"What? You can't do that!" He paused in the process of seating himself, and turned towards her.

"Yes, I can, and I will," she retorted hotly.

"I was right," he said. "You are having an affair with Favian Drake."

"How hard is it to believe that I am not like you?" she demanded. "You may think it is perfectly acceptable to bed someone to whom you are not married, but I do not."

"So you intend to marry him, then?"

"Yes," she said, "if he will still have me."

"But what about me?" he said. "What about our business partnership?"

"We can achieve that without marriage."

"No. You cannot do this. I will not allow you to break this contract." He grabbed her by the shoulders, forcing her to look at him, before bending his head and kissing her savagely. She struggled against him, but it was the voice from the doorway that made him pull away.

"Unhand her this instant." Father's voice was loud and angry. "I have been completely deceived in you, Geoffrey Beaumont." Geoffrey pulled away and ran a hand through his hair, giving Cathryn a sheepish grin before turning to her father.

"I have no idea to what you could be referring," he said. "Should I not be allowed to kiss my future wife?"

Cathryn opened her mouth to retort, but her father held up his hand.

"You know perfectly well to what I am referring, and it has nothing to do with you kissing Cathryn, as shameful as that is. I suppose she has already given you the news that she has chosen another, but even if she has not, there is no way I could allow this marriage to proceed."

"Ah," said Geoffrey, the color draining from his face. "So that is the way of it, then?"

"Yes," said Father. "You can find your own way out." Cathryn watched in growing confusion as Geoffrey nodded and left the room.

"What was all that about?" she asked.

"Geoffrey Beaumont is bankrupt," said Father. "He made some unwise investments, using his business as collateral, and has lost everything."

"Oh! How dreadful."

"Yes, indeed. Thankfully we were not too deep in with him, but if the marriage had gone ahead, we would have lost everything along with him."

"That explains his sudden desire for a quick wedding."

"Is that what he wanted? Perhaps it is a good thing Favian Drake crossed your path when he did, although I was not pleased about it last night."

"What will happen to Geoffrey?"

"The debt collectors will be after him for everything he has. He will have to hire out his services to earn some money. But do not waste your thoughts worrying for him. Men like Geoffrey Beaumont always land on their feet." Cathryn nodded, recognizing the truth in his words. Father walked towards the door, pausing at the entrance. "Bring your ledgers and notes to my study, and let's review what you have been doing."

CHAPTER THIRTY

Favian did not come the first day, nor the second or third. On the fourth day there was a small tap on the door, and Hannah announced that she had a visitor.

"Master Drake?"

"No. She gave her name as Madame Drake."

Cathryn looked at Hannah in surprise.

"Thank you."

She made her way slowly down the stairs. If Margaret was visiting, it could only mean bad news. Perhaps Favian did not want to see her. The red dragon scale lay on her chest, and she placed her hand over it. She pushed the door open and walked into the parlor.

"My dear," Margaret said, walking towards Cathryn and taking her by the hand. "I felt I needed to come and see you to explain."

"Explain?"

"Your note arrived a few days ago," Margaret said, "and I took the liberty of opening it. I hope you don't mind, but you see, Favian is away and I did not want you to be waiting for a response."

"Favian is away? Where has he gone?"

"I do not have an answer to that, my dear. All I can tell you is that he returned about two weeks ago, but before we had a chance to talk to him, he was gone again. He left nothing to indicate his direction, or how long his absence would be." She paused for a moment, watching Cathryn intently. "Cathryn, please forgive my inquisitiveness, but I need to ask you — why do you wish to see Favian?" Cathryn stared at Margaret in surprise, and she gave a sympathetic smile. "What I mean to say is, do you wish to tell Favian to leave you in peace?" Cathryn turned away, watching as people hurried past the window.

"No, I … uh … I want to apologize for … not … for being a coward."

"You do understand that Favian is … not like other men?"

"You mean that he is a dragon? Yes, I do know that."

"And you can accept that?" she asked.

"It came as rather a shock, at first," Cathryn replied with a sigh. She turned to look at Margaret. "I'm afraid I reacted rather poorly. Favian lost patience in the end. It was only after he was gone that I realized I should listen to my heart. I thought I could explain that to him, but …"

"Don't despair," Margaret said gently. "Favian will return. This is new to him as well."

"But what if he doesn't want me anymore?" Cathryn whispered.

"Favian loves you," Margaret said, "and no matter how angry he may be now, he will return." She lifted the pendant hanging around Cathryn's neck, holding it in her open palm. "This alone tells me that Favian will return. The gift of a dragon scale is more precious than any amount of gold or jewels. A dragon does not lose his scales the way a bird may lose a feather. It needs to be wrenched off, and once it is gone, that spot will be forever vulnerable. Favian has given you something of infinite value, my dear, and it was not lightly given." She dropped the pendant and smiled at

Cathryn. "But perhaps we can help things along. Aaron knows Favian better than anyone, and he will know where to look for him."

"I doubt Aaron will want to help," Cathryn said. "He does not like me very much."

"Nonsense," Margaret said briskly. "Aaron has no problem with you personally — just a problem with his humanity in general. But despite his disparagement of love as nothing more than a weakness, he does love Favian, more than anyone else in this world. He will do anything for his cousin, including finding him and bringing him home to the one he loves."

"Thank you," said Cathryn softly.

"Favian loves you, Cathryn," Margaret assured her. "Whatever may happen, and however long it takes, do not stop believing in that love."

As day after day passed, Cathryn found herself thinking back to Margaret's words. Surely if Favian loved her, he would not stay away so long. It seemed like a lifetime had passed when Hannah tapped on the door to her chambers before slowly opening it.

"You have a visitor, Mistress," she said.

"Master Drake?" asked Cathryn.

"Well, yes, Master Drake is his name, but not the one you are hoping for."

"Mistress," said Aaron with a smile as she slowly entered the room. She drew in a sharp breath at his friendly demeanor. With a smile, the man was actually quite handsome, she thought.

"Master Drake," she greeted with a nod.

"My apologies for this unexpected visit, but Margaret felt it would help to set your mind at ease if you know that I bear you no ill will."

"Ill will?" Cathryn repeated in confusion.

"Yes." Aaron turned away with a sigh and went to stare out the thick, leaded window. "I'm afraid my presence

163

caused you some distress when you were at Drake Manor. For that I apologize." He turned back to face her again. "I have held the society of humans in disdain for a very long time, Mistress, but Favian has been attempting to convince me that I was too hasty in my judgment, and perhaps he is right."

He took a few steps towards Cathryn, pausing when she flinched. "Love does not come easily to any of our kind, Mistress. Although we wear a guise of humanity, we remain creatures of the wild, powerful, predatory and worthy of fear. We have no need for warmth, or shelter, or food cultivated by humans. People run from us in fear, and we can smell it, revel in it. It is an intoxicating thing, knowing you hold the lives of so many within a single fiery breath." Cathryn stared at him, both terrified and awed at his words. "There is only one thing that makes us weak, and that is love for humans. And I am beginning to see that within that weakness, there is an element of strength. That love can serve to anchor us to who we are, beyond the beast. It makes us human." He paused as Cathryn watched him. "I know where to look for Favian, Mistress," he said. "I will remind him of his need for love, as he has reminded me so many times."

"Thank you," she said, taking a step towards him. "And please, call me Cathryn."

"Favian told me that you had strength of character," he said with a smile.

"I'm afraid I have not shown much strength of character lately," she replied with regret. "I was terrified when I realized what Favian was." Aaron nodded.

"Yes, so Favian told me, and I hold myself responsible. Again, my apologies."

"No," she said. "I was a coward. Please just find Favian so I can at least tell him how sorry I am."

"I will, Mistress … Cathryn." He held his palm towards her. "May I?" Cathryn looked at the outstretched hand for a moment before placing her own within his. Very slowly he brought her hand to his lips, barely brushing it with a kiss before releasing it again. "Good day, Cathryn," he said, and quickly strode out the door.

CHAPTER THIRTY-ONE

Cathryn was distracted. Surely Aaron should have found Favian by now. Every morning she went riding and every afternoon she spent at the warehouse, but these activities were not enough to keep her mind off the one person she longed to see.

A few days after Aaron's visit, she was called to her father's study.

"I have a meeting this afternoon with a clothier interested in pursuing a business relationship with a wool merchant," he said. "I would like you to come with me to meet him."

"Of course, Father," Cathryn said. "What is his name?"

"Master Grant. He is a friend of Tom Bradshaw's."

Master Grant was short and portly, with a balding crown and fleshly jowls. He had a kind face and a friendly smile, and Cathryn found she liked the man, despite her urge to shudder when he grasped her hand in his own warm, moist palms. He had been in the cloth industry for more than thirty years, and she listened as her father asked him questions about the business. It was clear from his answers, and the way he framed his questions, that he was very familiar with all aspects of the wool and cloth industry. They had spent more than two hours with the man by the time they rose to leave, and he turned to Cathryn with a smile as they walked towards the door.

"I have a son around your age," he said. "You will meet him soon should we pursue this relationship, since he is actively involved in the business. You have a lot of common — both of you are only children, raised without a mother."

"Really?" said Cathryn, her smile hiding her dismay.

"Yes, indeed," Master Grant replied. "He's recently become betrothed, so perhaps you will give us the pleasure of your company when we celebrate the exchange of vows."

"Oh, yes, that would be wonderful," said Cathryn. "Is the betrothal a business alliance?"

"A business alliance? No, indeed! When my wife died her cousin came to live with us. Dame Turner is a fine woman, very adept at keeping us all under control." His gaze turned inward for a moment, and Cathryn saw him shudder. "A fine woman," he repeated, bringing his attention back to Cathryn. "Her daughter Amelia is a lovely girl, very quiet and demure. She and Robert have loved each other from a young age. The only delay to the marriage was due to Dame Turner's, eh, reluctance, at seeing Amelia marry too young."

"How old is she?" asked Cathryn.

"How old? Oh. Um, seven and twenty."

Cathryn smiled to herself as she went down the stairs, stepping into the waiting carriage.

"I like him," she said to her father as the carriage lurched into motion.

"I do too," Father replied. "But before I enter into any further business arrangements, I would like his records inspected by a lawyer, and a proper contract drawn up."

"That," said Cathryn, "is an excellent plan."

The next few days were spent in consultation with a lawyer, and further meetings with Master Grant, but Cathryn struggled to keep her mind on the business at hand. Why had Favian not come? She could not keep the question from plaguing her mind. As the days passed she could feel the lassitude bearing down on her, smothering her like a blanket. Once, she came upon Hannah and Father in earnest conversation, but the conversation ceased as soon as Cathryn walked into the room. They continued to stare at her, however, and after a moment, she turned around and left the room.

More days dragged by. The full heat of summer had arrived, one endless day of heat after another. At night Cathryn flung the shutters wide open, desperate to feel the air circulating through the room, but she would lie awake, hot and sweaty. When she did finally succumb to sleep, it offered little in the way of rest as dragons plagued her dreams.

Another market day rolled around, and Cathryn stood at her window watching the crowds milling towards the market square. She had lost track of the days since she had seen Aaron, and she felt a sense of despair creeping into her heart. Had Favian given up on her altogether? As she watched the milling crowds, she was seized with a sudden determination to join the throng. Even if only for a few hours, she would put her torment behind her and enjoy the morning. Securing her purse to her waist, she picked up a basket and headed out the door, following the people heading toward the cobbled square in the center of town.

A visiting merchant caught Cathryn's eye, and she headed to his small stall to inspect the finely crafted wooden sculptures that decorated his table, picking up one of an eagle in flight. The craftsman had captured the form so well, Cathryn could imagine the bird taking flight from her hand as she watched.

"This is beautiful," she said with a smile. "Do you have other animals?"

"Yes, Mistress," said the man, laying down a small block of wood he had been working on. "Over here I have a wolf, and somewhere ... ah, yes, here it is ... is a rabbit."

"Lovely," said Cathryn, leaning forward to inspect the pieces. "What about other creatures?"

"What kind of creatures do you have in mind, Mistress?" asked the man, turning his brown eyes on her.

"Um, well, how about a dragon?"

"A dragon, hmm? No, I don't have any dragons, but I do have a lion." Cathryn looked at it politely, before placing it back down with a smile. She was about to turn away when she felt a shiver run down the back of her spine. Spinning on her heel, she scanned the crowds, certain she was being watched. All around her people were bustling from one stall to the other, and the market buzzed with activity. Peasant wives haggled with vegetable sellers, ladies inspected cloth, and men held swords up to the light, their fingers running over the smooth and deadly surfaces. Children chased each other, their hands sticky from buns and other sweetened delights as they wound through the throngs. No-one gave Cathryn the slightest notice. Taking a firm grip on her basket, Cathryn pushed her way back into the flow of people, her attention fixed on a stall on the opposite side. The crowd thinned as she approached her goal, and she quickened her step. She was almost there when a warm hand clamped around her arm, pulling her into a darkened passageway. Confused, she looked up into a pair of dark blue eyes, burning with faint spots of yellow.

"Favian," she gasped, "you're here! I've been waiting for you. Did you get my note? When did you return?"

Favian released the hold on her arm, and took a step backwards, his arms crossed over his chest.

"I believe you wanted to see me," he said coolly. His tone brought Cathryn up short, and she took in a deep breath, eyeing him carefully.

"Yes," she said. She looked back at the crowded marketplace, then slowly turned back to him. "Why were you waiting for me here? Why didn't you come to the house? Where have you been?"

"I understand the nuptial agreement with Geoffrey Beaumont has been annulled," he said.

"Yes?"

"I also understand this annulment is a result of a change in Beaumont's circumstances."

"What? No. Where did you hear that?"

"I got the news from your friend Peggy last week."

"Last week?" she gasped. "You have been in town for a whole week? And you never came to see me? Surely you knew I wanted to see you? Why?"

"I've been watching you," he said, leaning a little closer. "You've been very busy, haven't you?"

Cathryn stared at him in astonishment.

"Yes," she hissed, "busy keeping myself distracted." She watched as the yellow flecks in his eyes flared for a brief moment. "Why did you not come to see me?" she asked again.

"I knew what you had to say. Since you were no longer marrying Geoffrey, you had decided to accept my offer. But Cathryn, I refuse to accept second place." He leaned closer, bringing his face to within a few inches of hers. "You would not break the contract for my sake, but you expect me to accept the scraps."

"Scraps?" she demanded incredulously. "You consider my love for you mere 'scraps'? I had already broken the contract when I heard the news about Geoffrey. I was ready to give you the whole meal, Favian Drake." She turned on her heel, but Favian caught her by the arm.

"I don't believe you," he said. She took in a deep breath, then turned to look into his face.

"Your belief or disbelief does not change the truth,

Favian," she said. "I refuse to continue this conversation here, but you can call on me at home if you wish." Shaking her arm free of his hand, she stepped out of the shadows and turned in the direction that led home. She heard Favian fall into step beside her, but ignored him, instead lengthening her stride as she marched in silence down the lane, her eyes straight ahead. She could feel him watching her as they walked, his long stride easily matching hers, and she lifted her chin slightly. A glint of silver caught Cathryn's eye, and she darted a quick sideways glance to see the sleeve of his tunic pulled up to reveal a silver bangle on his wrist. She quickly looked forward once more.

They reached the house in silence, and Favian followed her as she pushed the door open and walked into the long hall of the house. She paused a moment to put down the basket, before swiftly walking to the parlor, Favian still close on her heels. As they entered the room, Favian closed the door quietly behind him as she turned to look at him for the first time since the market.

"How could you?" she said. "You knew I was waiting to see you, and yet you did nothing to relieve my anxiety. Why?"

"You think I should come whenever you beckon?" he retorted. "Your contract with Geoffrey may now be annulled, but you would not break it for my sake. And yet you expect me to hang around your feet like a lap dog!"

"I did break it for your sake!" she shouted. "I told Geoffrey that I would not marry him before I knew about his bankruptcy!"

"Dammit, Cathryn! How can I believe you? You have pushed me away at every opportunity." She took a step back as he strode towards her. "You are destroying me!"

She saw the flames flare into his eyes in the moment before his hands wrapped around her neck in an unbreakable clasp, and his lips descended on hers, hard and unrelenting. She struggled against his hold, but he slipped a hand down her back and pulled her even closer, molding his body to hers. His grip around her neck loosened, and his kiss softened, coaxing a response from her, and she felt her resolve slipping as his tongue teased hers. She heard a soft moan, startled to realize that it had come from her, and he buried his hand into her hair, stroking and teasing her as her hands slid around his back. He pulled away from her lips and trailed kisses down the side of her neck as she held him close, before once more claiming her mouth. She was breathless when he pulled away, his forehead resting on hers.

"Never before have I been so tormented," he said. "I cannot bear the thought of walking away from you, but cannot accept second place. I want you to be completely mine, and want your complete acceptance of what I am." His eyes blazed into hers as he spoke, his heat pressing through her clothes and into her skin.

"There is no second place, Favian," she said. "You already have all of me."

"I wish I could believe that," he said softly. A sound at the door made them draw apart hastily, and Favian closed his eyes as Father walked into the room.

"Cathryn," he said, looking at Favian as he slowly opened his deep blue eyes. "I see we have a guest."

"Yes, Father. This is Favian Drake."

"Hmm," said Father, subjecting Favian to intense scrutiny. "Favian Drake, eh? About time you showed up! I've been asking around town about you. You seem to be a bit of a mystery, although I have not heard anything averse about your character. I was not very happy when Cathryn informed me of her intention to break the betrothal agreement with Geoffrey Beaumont, but it would appear fate made a timely intervention." Favian threw Cathryn a quick look that expressed both regret and satisfaction, before returning his attention to Father, who had not paused. "When are you planning to exchange vows?"

"One week hence," Favian said, "and then return to Drake Manor."

"Drake Manor? In one week?" protested Father, turning to face Cathryn. "What about the business? I need to return to court at the end of summer." He turned back towards Favian. "Do you intend to reside permanently at Drake Manor?"

"We have not yet discussed that," Cathryn quickly interposed before Favian could respond. "I will not abandon you while you still need my assistance, but Felix is quite capable of handling things for you."

"Hmph. This is what comes from marrying for love," he said darkly. "You turn your back on the things that are important."

Beside her Cathryn could feel Favian tense, and she reached out her hand to him, wrapping her fingers around his as Father watched with a frown. She took a deep breath to steady her tone.

"Although you consider my actions self-serving, Father, I consider my future happiness to be of even greater importance," she said. "I am not turning my back on you or the business, but you must understand that my place from this moment forward will be with Favian, wherever that may be." She cast a quick glance at Favian, catching his smile of approval. Father looked at her from beneath lowered eyebrows.

"Very well. I can see further argument now would be futile. However this discussion is not at an end, daughter. And," he added, turning to look at Favian, "I would like a few words with you. Come and see me in my study before you leave."

"Of course," Favian said as the older man strode out of the room.

"One week?" Cathryn said as the door closed, leaving them alone once again. "I thought you were doubting my love for you."

"I would marry you today, fool that I am, although it appears I owe you an apology for thinking you broke with Beaumont because of his bankruptcy. I should have trusted you." He looked away for a moment, his expression pensive, before returning his gaze to her. "I also owe you an apology for the things I said in the woods. I said them because I was angry and wanted to shock you, and although they had an element of truth, I was exaggerating greatly. Later I was deeply ashamed, which just fueled my anger. Being angry with you allowed me to justify my own despicable behavior, and even when you gave me proof of your regard for me, my mind refused to countenance it." He held up his hand to reveal the bangle. "But deep within my beastly heart, I could not deny my love for you, or that you loved me. I've worn this every day since that day in the woods," he said. His expression was filled with remorse as he gazed at her. "Please forgive me," he whispered.

"Of course I forgive you," she said, wrapping her hands around his neck and pulling his face down towards hers. "You're only human, after all," she finished with a grin. His laugh was muffled as he brushed his lips against hers.

"I love you," he said. He pulled away a few moments later, but when he started to tug the bangle from his wrist, she stopped him.

"I know this is something usually worn by a lady, but you gave me something, and I want you to keep it as a token of my love for you. It doesn't contain a part of me, like your pendant does, but it does carry my love."

"Give me a lock of your hair," he said, "and I will meld it into the metal."

"It will just fall out," she said, but she crossed over to a basket of needlework and withdrew a small pair of scissors. He smiled and walked to where she stood, and carefully separating a few strands of her hair, he took the scissors from her hand and snipped them off. Tugging the bangle from his wrist, he held it in his palm.

"Ready?" he asked.

"For what?" she said, confused.

"For this," he replied, bringing the bangle up to his mouth and gently blowing. A stream of flame burst from between his lips, and Cathryn pulled back in shock, then leaned forward to look as Favian gently pressed her hair into the softening metal, creating ridges along the edges of the filigree. Turning to a pitcher of wine, Favian dropped the bangle into the liquid, where it sizzled and hissed.

"Wine?" she said.

"I needed something to cool the metal, and since there is no pail of water, I used what was available," he said with a grin. He fished the bangle out of the pitcher and shook off the drops of liquid. Taking it from his hand, Cathryn inspected it closely. It was still warm, but no longer soft.

"How does a dragon wear a bangle?" she asked as she wrapped the jewelry around Favian's outstretched wrist.

"Come fly with me," he said, "and I'll show you."

"Fly with you? In town?"

"No," he said. "While I go chat with your father, ride out to the oak tree in the meadow. I will find you when I am done." She smiled as he headed out the door.

CHAPTER THIRTY-TWO

Cathryn slid off her horse, her eyes searching the heavens. The sky remained empty, however, and she returned her attention to her horse, using a long length of soft cloth to hobble her mount. A flash of light high in the sky caught her attention, and she looked up to see a dark shadow against the blue, growing larger as it approached the earth. As it grew closer, she could see enormous wings opened wide, with the form of a man hanging between them. He dropped down right in front of her, his bare chest mere inches away as his feet touched the ground. In his hand he held his tunic, and he threw it onto the ground near Morana.

"Come," he said, wrapping his arms around her. The ground disappeared from beneath her feet before she even had a chance to respond.

"Where are we going?" she managed to choke out as the air rushed past her face. She wrapped her arms around his back and held tightly, her face paling as she saw how high they were climbing. Favian leaned back and smiled into her face in amusement.

"I won't let you fall," he said. "We are going somewhere

completely private."

"Oh," was all she could manage to say before the wind sucked her breath away.

The land beneath grew distant as Favian climbed into the clouds, his powerful wings flexing through the air with ease, the muscles in his back taut against his skin. With each beat the wings brushed against Cathryn's hand as she clung to his waist, and she cautiously stretched out her fingers to stroke the smooth, silky surface of his wings as they carried them aloft. At her touch, he bent his wings inward slightly, bringing them closer to his body and her reaching fingers. His arms tightened around her, and his face dropped into her hair as he stroked her back.

"No wings," she whispered into his shoulder.

"If I wanted a woman with wings, I could have had one," he said, his mouth near her ear. "It is you I want, and you are perfect just the way you are, fully human." She smiled, and stretched her hand a little further.

He brought them down to land on a small rocky outcrop at the top of a mountain peak. The air was much colder this high, and she shivered when Favian stepped away from her.

"Are you not cold?" she asked.

"I have fire flowing through my veins," he replied. "No, I'm not cold. In fact, this is the perfect temperature." He laughed at her grimace. "I'll keep you warm," he promised. Taking her by the hand he sat her down at the edge of the rock, and sitting behind her, pulled her between his legs, dropping his feet over the edge of the ledge. Tentatively, Cathryn followed suit, pulling back when she saw how far a drop it was, then leaning against Favian's chest as his arms wrapped around her. She snuggled into his warmth with a sigh.

"Comfortable?" he asked with a laugh.

"Mmm, yes," she said. "Nothing like a dragon's hide to keep you warm."

"Just as long as you don't seek to remove the hide from the dragon, all will be well," he said, nuzzling her neck.

"Why did Father want to speak with you?" she asked.

"He wanted to assure himself that he was not letting his daughter marry a monster."

"And was he satisfied?"

"I'm not sure 'satisfied' would be the correct term, but I think I convinced him I was not about to lock you away in a dungeon."

"You didn't tell him what you are, did you?" she asked.

"Absolutely not," he said. His tone was serious, and she turned to look at him. "We guard the secret of who we are very jealously, Cathryn. It is very important that you never tell anyone what I am. The knowledge of our existence can be a significant danger to humans."

"Why?"

"Because humans fear dragons more than any other creature. They would seek us out in an effort to kill us if they knew we existed, but the only way a dragon can be killed by humans is if he allows that to happen. Instead of a dead dragon, you would have dozens of dead humans."

"Why would a dragon allow himself to be killed?" she asked. Favian gazed into her face for a long moment before looking away with a sigh.

"There is usually only one reason. Love."

"Love? I don't understand."

"Aaron saw both of his parents being killed by humans. His mother was killed by a jealous lover, and in his anguish, his father did nothing to defend himself when the villagers came after him. He was in his dragon form and the villagers believed he was responsible for Eleanor's death."

"That's terrible."

"It is. And it is the reason why Aaron has tried to deny his humanity. But many humans lost their lives that day as well, so the agony was not confined to dragons." Cathryn turned back to view the panoramic vista once more.

"Do you know Aaron came to see me? He said he would find you."

"Yes, I know." Favian pulled his arms away and leaned back on his hands. "He found me as he said he would."

"Where?" she asked.

"I would prefer not to talk about it," he said. "It was not my finest hour." She opened her mouth to argue, but then stopped when she caught sight of his expression, returning her gaze to the distant mountains as he wrapped his arms around her again.

"Favian?" she said.

"Hmm?"

"That day in the woods ... you said ..." Favian groaned into her hair as her words trailed off.

"I wondered when this would come up. I said some things that I will always regret."

"So ...?" she prompted, reluctant to put her question into words.

"So the answer is yes, sometimes, and no."

"Yes, sometimes, and no? What does that mean?"

"Yes, dragons eat human flesh; I sometimes enjoy it; and no, I would never think of you in that way."

"You would never want to eat me?" she asked dryly, crossing her arms against her chest. "That is ... comforting."

"Cathryn, I am a dragon. Not a human. A dragon. I may have a human mother, but I am still a dragon. Nothing can ever change that." He lifted his hand and held it out in front of her as a flame flared up from his palm. "I am created from fire. I may wear a human guise, but that does not change who I am. Dragons need the occasional human flesh to survive. But that does not mean I view you as my next meal. I love you." He buried his nose in her hair and breathed in deeply. "I carry your scent in my mind, but it is not the scent of my prey. It is the scent of my lover." Cathryn shivered at his words, her emotions warring within her. She turned within his arms to look at him.

"And what about when you are a dragon? What do I smell like then?"

"I am always a dragon. Taking on my natural form does not mean I view you any differently. I still want to feel you, and breathe in your scent, and love you. I want to touch you, and feel you touching me too." At his words, Cathryn could feel a twist of warmth snake through her belly. She lifted her hand to his face and stroked his cheeks as the yellow flecks in his eyes started to glow.

"Why is it that your eyes are sometimes blue, and other times filled with flame?"

"I was born with blue eyes," he said. "But the stronger my emotions, the closer the flames rise to the surface. I can usually keep them in check, but with you," he shrugged, "you are already too much a part of me for me to hide my feelings." He smiled as the blue of his eyes started to burn away, leaving only black pupils surrounded by brightly burning flames.

"Your skin feels so much warmer," she whispered.

"That's because my human skin is wearing thin. The flames are closer to the surface."

"Show me the dragon," she said. He stared down at her for a moment, and then slowly pulled himself away from her.

"You will have to close your eyes," he said. "There is an explosion of light that your eyes cannot yet handle."

"Yet?"

"I'll explain soon," he assured her. "Now turn away and cover your eyes." She did as she was bade, but even so, she could see the light spread around and then suddenly disappear. She pulled her hands from her face and turned around to look at the creature standing before her. Her heart pounded in her chest as she stared at the huge beast. She drew back slightly when he raised sharply curving claws, then gave a nervous laugh when she saw her silver bangle wrapped around a sharp talon.

"So that's how you wear it," she said as he dropped the claws back to the ground.

"You're still scared of me," he said with a sigh.

"No," she replied. "It is just that you are so ... big." Slowly he dropped down onto the ground, folding his legs beneath him and dropping his head down to her eye level. His wings were folded against his back, but he opened them, spreading them to their fullest extent.

"Come, my love," he said, "I know how much you admire my wings. Come touch them." She eyed him dubiously, and he shifted himself slightly, bringing one of his wings closer to where she stood. With a deep breath, she stepped towards him and ran a hand over the taut span of his wing, watching as the smooth surface rippled with her touch, glimmering in the light. A framework of bone fanned out from his back and ran through the wings, supporting the huge appendages. The bones ended in sharp points at various intervals along the outer edges of his wings, and she ran her hand over them, feeling the pointed tips.

"I love it when you touch me," he breathed, a stream of flame flowing from his mouth as he watched her over his shoulder. She moved along the edge of his wings tentatively, and he slowly brought his tail around, curling it around her legs. She glanced back at his face, and then reached down to touch the tail, running her fingers along the thick scaly length, following the curve he had made around her legs. When she could reach no further, he slowly unwound it, giving her space to trace it towards his body. The tail was armed with sharp, bony spikes, and she ran her finger over one of the tips. It was as sharp as it looked, and she pulled her finger away to look at the blood staining her skin.

"Cathryn?" he said softly, and she turned towards him, holding up her finger. "Come here," he said, his voice dropping even lower. She looked at her finger, and then back at the rows of sharp teeth lining his mouth. Slowly she walked around to his face, and after another momentary pause, lifted her hand. Slowly, his bright gaze holding hers, he flicked his forked, reptilian tongue at her finger, first licking off the drop of blood and then slowly trailing it down the finger's length. He closed his eyes and shuddered, pulling in his tongue and closing his mouth. A moment passed before he opened them again.

"I've tasted your blood," he said, "now you should taste mine."

"No," she said, stumbling back a step.

"Cathryn." His voice was low and demanding, and she stopped to stare at him. She nodded after a moment, and he turned his head, pointing with his talon to a spot near his underbelly. "Do you see that gap?" he asked. Cathryn moved closer to look, and saw that there was a scale missing in the space he had pointed out. She lifted her hand to her pendant as her gaze flew to his. He nodded, and then using his talon, pierced the skin exposed by the missing scale. A large drop of blood welled up in the spot when he pulled his talon away, and Cathryn stared at it, mesmerized. She stretched out a hand to catch the liquid as it slowly fell towards the ground, and it splashed onto her palm. It was warm, she noticed, just like the rest of him. She lifted her gaze to his and raised her hand, bringing her palm to her mouth and licking off the single drop of blood. Her eyes widened as the blood hit her taste buds. It was unlike anything she had expected — sweet, like strong mulled wine — and even though it had been just one drop, it weaved its way through her, exploding through her veins.

Without another word, Favian wrapped the smooth side of his tail around her and lifted her onto his back. She gasped, and then threw her arms around his neck as he rose into the air. He spiraled up towards the heavens, and then dived down toward the ground. The speed took Cathryn's breath away, and she could not even scream as the earth got closer at an alarming rate. When she was sure they were about to crash, he pulled himself back up into the air, spiraling back up towards the mountain peak where they had been sitting.

"What was that?" she gasped when she was finally able to draw in a breath. He laughed, spewing out flames that warmed the air around her.

"You are marrying a dragon, my love," he said. "I thought I should show you just what you are in for."

"If that is what I am in for, then perhaps I should reconsider," she retorted. He laughed again as he landed once more on the rocky ledge.

"Cover your eyes, my love," he said. She turned around and covered her eyes, turning back again as the light faded. He was pulling on his trousers, and she felt the blood rush into her cheeks. He walked up to her and pulled her into his arms. "No need to be embarrassed," he said. "Soon it will all be yours to enjoy." The blush deepened as he dropped his lips to hers, capturing them in a deep kiss. He led her back to the edge of the ledge once more, again wrapping himself around her to keep her warm.

"There's more you need to know about marrying a dragon," he said as she leaned back against his chest.

"Oh?" she said, bending her head to look up at him.

"In order for a dragon marriage to be recognized, there needs to be a blood-binding ceremony."

"What's that?" she asked.

"It is an exchange of blood."

"What kind of exchange?"

"Well," he said, "we will have to drink each other's blood."

"And how exactly do we do that?" she asked warily.

"I will spill your blood into a cup, and you will do the same."

"And there will be witnesses?"

"Yes. And the ceremony will be conducted by the Dragon Master."

"Dragons have a master?"

"Yes, like a clan chief."

"And where does the Dragon Master live?"

"Actually, you've already met him," said Favian. "The Dragon Master is Aaron."

"Aaron? Aaron is the Dragon Master? But how is that possible?"

Favian shrugged. "The Dragon Master has to fight for the position, but Aaron's father was master before him, which made it easier for him to win the support of the clan. There was only one other contender, and he did not survive the contest."

"So I need to drink your blood? I think I can manage that — I've tasted it already." She turned to look at him suspiciously. "You did that on purpose, didn't you?" Favian shrugged, unrepentant.

"I didn't plan it, if that's what you mean, but I took the opportunity when it presented itself. It seemed to me that you might accept the news better if you had already tasted my blood." He grinned. "Did you like it?"

"Why do we need to drink each other's blood?" she asked, ignoring the question.

"The drinking of blood binds us together. Your blood will be in my veins, and mine will be in yours. But there is an added benefit for you. Drinking my blood will imbue you with some dragon qualities."

"Am I going to start growing a tail?" she asked, only partly in jest.

"No," he smiled, "and no wings either. Your senses will be heightened, so you won't need to cover your eyes when I change form, you will heal faster and you will live longer."

"Live longer?" she looked at him in confusion for a moment, and he waited as comprehension soon followed. "How old are you?" she demanded.

"About one hundred," he said.

"About?"

"Ninety-five," he clarified. She closed her eyes for a moment, trying to accept this new revelation.

"How old is your mother?" she whispered.

"A hundred and twenty-seven," he replied. The air seemed to suddenly turn to liquid as she struggled to pull it into her lungs, and she sucked at it in short, shallow gulps as the blood pounded in her ears, creating a roaring sound that blocked out everything else. He wrapped his arms around her and held her close. "Breathe deeply," he said softly, and somehow she heard him through the roar. She gulped, forcing herself to suck the air into her lungs, until finally she felt her pulse starting to steady. "All right?" he asked. She nodded, still uncertain of her voice, and took in another deep breath.

"How long will I live?" she asked when she finally felt she could breathe.

"Longer than humans, but not as long as me. The more blood you drink, the longer you will live." He watched her face intently as he spoke. "It is a lot to take in, I know. Are you all right?"

She nodded. "Yes, I'm ... fine. At least, I will be." He waited in silence, watching her as she stared unfocused into the distance. Finally she turned to him with a small smile. "We've discussed the ceremony, and the, uh, benefits to me. Perhaps we should talk about what happens after."

"After?"

"Yes. This has all been quite a shock for my father. Apart from him, there is no-one that knows the business as I do, and from the time I was young, my father has groomed me to take over the reins. I cannot abandon him now, during the busiest season."

"Hmm," he said thoughtfully. "As long as I am with you, I will not stop you from doing what you believe you should. After all, I will have you for many more years than

185

your father will. But I will not tolerate it if the business becomes more important than me. You already know that I can become quite unreasonable when aroused to jealousy. And," he added with a grim smile, "a jealous dragon is never a pretty sight." Cathryn nodded.

"This is important to me, but not as important as you. I will do this only if I know I have your support. But if I continue to work with my father, then he will have something to leave his grandchildren." She smiled up at Favian impishly as he laughed.

"A masterful maid of manipulation," he said. "No wonder I love you." He bent down to nibble playfully at her ear, but she swatted him away.

"We haven't finished."

"Enough talking," he coaxed. "Give me a kiss."

"No. We still need to plan where we are going to live."

"As long as I am with you, I can live anywhere," he said, his breath tickling her cheek. "A cave in the mountains, perhaps. Under the stars in a field? No?" he said when she started to pull away. "Drake Manor? We can have the wing above the kitchen, and build on additional rooms when the need arises."

"But Aaron has those chambers," she said, her line of thought momentarily distracted.

"He has plenty of his own estates," said Favian. "He only stays at Drake Manor to be close to us."

"But we shouldn't force him away."

"There are plenty of places Aaron can sleep, and if he wishes to have a bed, he can use the guest chambers."

"Regardless, Drake Manor is too far away from town."

"It is only a short flight," he protested.

"Yes, you are right. I am happy to inform my father about our mode of transportation."

"Very well," he said with an exaggerated sigh. "We can rent a house close to town. Not too close, mind you, but close enough to satisfy your father."

"Thank you," she said. She turned to look at him. "I know many other husbands would not show such generosity to their wives."

"I love you," he said in surprise. "Why would I not want to see you happy?" He pulled her to her feet. "Ready to go?" he asked. He stood behind her, and as she nodded yes, he wrapped his arms across her chest and threw both of them off the rock face, tangling his feet around hers as they left the ground. The wind whipped a scream from her mouth, and he buried his lips in her hair as it flew around his face. "I won't let you go, I give you my word," he said. His wings spread like a canopy above them, and Cathryn could see the red tips as they curved through the air, strong and powerful. His arms held her close, and she clenched her hands around them, taking comfort in the tight sinew and muscle that was taut beneath his skin. She was not about to perish, she realized, and as that thought took hold of her mind, her body began to relax. Slowly she began to loosen the death grip on his arms, opening her fingers one by one and letting her arms hang limp. She stretched out one arm to her side, and then the other, reaching with her fingers so they brushed against his wings.

She felt Favian smile into her hair, and a bubble of pure joy rose up within her. She laughed, reveling in the freedom of flying as his feet hooked more securely about hers. The pressure of the air around them pressed them together, and she could feel his chest against her back. Slowly, he drew one of his arms away from her chest and stretched his hand out along her arm, wrapping his fingers around hers as they reached her hand.

"I love you," he said into her ear.

"I love you too," she replied, but the words were whipped from her mouth and she wasn't sure he heard them. They were gliding through the air, his wings no longer beating, and she closed her eyes. All was silent, except the beating of her heart and the wind rushing by.

ABOUT THE AUTHOR

Linda K. Hopkins grew up in South Africa, but now lives in Calgary, Canada with her husband and two daughters. Head over to her website, www.lindakhopkins.com, to learn more about the author. Sign up for updates, and be among the first to hear about new releases. You can also follow her on Facebook at https://www.facebook.com/pages/LindaKHopkins/

OTHER BOOKS BY LINDA K. HOPKINS

Bound by a Dragon

Loved by a Dragon (Spring 2015)

CPSIA information can be obtained
at www.ICGtesting.com
Printed in the USA
LVOW04s1322160216

475331LV00025B/488/P